The Granny State
of Drumhumble

by

I.D.C. Hopkins

COPYRIGHT: I.D.C. Hopkins.

Contents

CHAPTER 1: LOST IN SPACE (or somewhere worse) 1
CHAPTER 2: The State of Granny. 10
CHAPTER 3: FRUGAL McDOUGAL. 30
CHAPTER 4: ONE-SIDED NEGOTIATIONS 41
CHAPTER 5: LIFE AT THE INN. 52
CHAPTER 6: TRYSTING THE NIGHT AWAY…Part One 58
CHAPTER 7: GENESIS (of sorts…Auto?) 76
CHAPTER 8: COURT 80
CHAPTER 9: THE NIGHT AWAY…at last…mibbe. 93
CHAPTER 10: GM v WWW… catchweight and no-contest 103
CHAPTER 11: ANIMAL (and bird) RESCUE 107
CHAPTER 12: ALL IS REVEALED (nearly) 113
CHAPTER 13: SECOND CHANCES AND MORE REVELATIONS 121
CHAPTER 14: EEDJITS DAY 133
CHAPTER 15: GOODBYE & HELLO (again). 137
CHAPTER 16: DEAL OR NO DEAL. 142
CHAPTER 17: NINE MONTHS LATER (near enough) 149
EPILOGUE come CODA 155
TRANSLATIONS, EXPLANATIONS, EXPANSIONS AND ASIDES.
.... 158

ACKNOWLEDGEMENTS:

1. EDITOR IN CHIEF: Linda Henderson. Thanks for all your 'hard love' (and incredible patience *inter* mucho *alia*).

2. FIRST READER: Wilson Bulloch. Thanks for always being first 'feedbacker' (and always encouraging.)

3. INSIGHTFUL READER: Graeme Hyslop. Thanks for your erudition (and good taste!)

4. READERS: Pam Airey; Campbell Cooper; Frank Donnelly; Gary Hopkins; Sheila Hopkins; Jean Kirk; Marlene Manson. Thank you each and every one for invaluable feedback.

5. ILUSTRATOR: Murray Leven. I just love your front cover.

6. DIGITAL TECHNICIAN: Hamish Leven. Don't ken how you do it (and don't want to!)

Dedication

To the memory of Russell Campbell without whom this novella could not have been written.

Drumhumble was originally a completed television sit com co-written with my friend, Russell, the best of company, and the truest of guys. The sit com is and always will be 'in development' by the tv company. But Russell is tragically gone. I miss you, Russell, and the host of laughs we had writing together.

The Granny State of Drumhumble

CHAPTER 1: LOST IN SPACE (or somewhere worse).

1.

Oh No

FROM NORFOLK TO no folk.

It had been a long, tiring, haul by car. Now he ached.

Walter Wilson Winston (aka WWW.) was not happy.

Walt was lost.

Walt was worried.

Walt was now in pain: first cramp then lumbago, now sciatica. He had to get out. Regardless.

In his beloved Mazda 5 after this 13 hour journey, the last 'comfort break' just outside Inverness long past, had left his 25 year-old unfit overweight body truly suffering.

Now his mind was unravelling.

The current scenery, or rather the lack of it, did nothing to help his unease, mounting now towards panic. Dismal dripping wet moor and more moor and then some more moor. . .Walt imagined the odd clump of rushes that failed to break up the relentless monotony as paint brushes discarded by landscape artists disgusted at the lack of interesting subject matter. Not even Constable or Turner could have done much with the occasional, roadside snow pole as the *only* noticeable feature in late October.

He knew he should get out the car and stretch but in the face of the relentless drizzle he decided to settle for fully reclining his seat after stopping in the next Passing Place on this single-track road. Walt wondered not for the first time about his Sat Nav's competence. This Sat Nav (*Nexus*) had been known to fail him before. And that was in *his flats* of East Anglia. This was *their high lands* of Scotland.

Nexus, as if osmotically needled, spoke at him, seemingly more strident, terse, higher-pitched than before; with 'her' nagging apparently abandoned – was 'she' starting to panic too?

'*No signal! Try later!*

Not for the first time he wondered if the more expensive car guidance systems included politeness, civility, or even decent manners. *Nexus* being bottom of the range and being a stranger to *please* and *thank you*' often added to Walt's alienation: reminding him of his loneliness and lack of a girlfriend as Nexus was as close to female companionship as Walt had come since leaving school seven years ago.

He knew deep down that he was being silly but now Panic's adrenaline flooded Walt's more rational synapses. The immediate peace and relief from the silence of his digital companion was quickly swamped by the question:

Where on earth am I?

He automatically grabbed his smart phone for the Internet, forgetting.

No connection. No bars. No alcohol. . .Walt often cracked bad puns when he panicked. He often panicked. Like right now. Walt could not function without the Internet neither at a personal and most certainly not at a business level.

He got out, licked away the drizzle, cursed his lot, sprung the boot and lifted the mockery of a spare tyre to unearth the crumpled, tattered fifteen year old *AA atlas - the 2035 Map of Great Britain* that the previous (third) owner had left in the boot.

He jumped back in the car and damply flicked the index to D and through. . .Dr. . .Drum. . .Drumhum. . .and as he feared his destination was unlisted.

Drumhumble.

2.

TIKBOX

Walt peered in vain again through the rain and mist. No signpost, no sign of anything. . .he wanted to speed up, to get to somewhere, anywhere, anywhere but this potholed, ice-rutted single track and the dismal sight that mocked his headlights and thwarted any speed above even normal urban crawl. Twenty was more than Plenty. '*Five to stay Alive*' he snorted and *barely achievable.* He silently cursed his conscience, his ambition and his big digital mouth.

Walt Winston founder, owner, sole proprietor and only worker of *TikBox* (patent pending) was if nothing, conscientious. Having no greater achievement than one A level (in computing), Walt had been a shelf stacker, check out assistant, call centre salesperson, waiter, and cleaner (night shift: permanent).

Enough merde he had thought at 24 and he decided to use his one skill for himself as no one else seemed to want it. On the shoulders of the giant *Trip Advisor*, Walt cocooned in his Norfolk bedroom, began to build his travel advice web site and intended empire.

TikBox.

With *Tik Box*, Walt just *knew* he was onto a winner. He now had three minor hotel chains signed up and a real Biggie waiting in the wings. All those lovely commissions for all those bookings through *TikBox*, would surpass, probably swallow his role model; at worst *Trip Advisor* would buy him out, buy him off, or just buy him. Then

The Granny State of Drumhumble

Walt would be rich. And finally get a girl. Maybe even one to love him --at first probably for his money but then, once she got to know the real Walter. . .He shivered with excitement. . .

Bang! Bloody pothole(s)! He braked, stopped, switched off the ersatz sports car's engine and half laughed, half cried. The Mazda 5, bought with his first decent profits. The sports car. Fourth hand but the only one affordable but still the chick magnet! Huh. . .As if. . .look where it had got him. Nowhere.

Now literally.

Walt peered through the ever-thickening mist, oblivious to the benefit of it obscuring the bleakness of the landscape and decided that there was nothing for it but continuing to drive slowly ahead. More slowly. Without stalling. There must eventually be some kind of signpost. . .

He was regretting being a one-man business. Perhaps he had bitten off more than he could chew now that the government were on the cusp of legislation: to further tighten the constraints on 'Advice Websites'. Especially those offering spurious, suspicious hospitality reviews.

Reviews like those of *The Drumhumble Inn*. They needed checking. Empirically, up close and personal. . .by the Boss.

Walt had known that his *TikBox* had to be different or it would never have got off the ground to soar then fly in the digital ether. Differentiate the Product -all the experts Walt had read had that one instruction in common. In addition to his nugatory cash incentives to reviewers and his novel ten-star rating system (not the 'normal' 1 to 5 where five was excellent and one was somewhat less than acceptable) Walt had claimed and promised on his website to guarantee 'no phoney reviews'. This had cost him expenses in time and travel but every suspicious, potentially rogue review he found he trumpeted, using it to boost his website's authenticity and attraction by exposing the bogus. It was better PR than he had a right to expect - fifty ten-star phoney reviews he had named, shamed, and scrubbed. Every one of them had the taint of unanimity. Consistency was a dead giveaway. One person's concept of glorious ten- star luxury was another person's idea of arrant one-star rip-off. Human nature's rich tapestry, Walt figured.

The *Drumhumble Inn's* mere *seven* total reviews would not normally have raised Walt's mental flag. Seven reviews, though consistent, did not meet his minimum quantity of ten, warranting action. But for one thing. They were *all negative*.

Each review was One Star. And on a *Ten* Star Scale.

Walt did not need to refer to them online. They were imprinted on his brain and they had accompanied him all the way from Norfolk often shutting out even *Nexus*. . .The 'best' ones – the top three played out between his ears now:

'On a one to a million rating system this dump would still NOT score one.'

'Better than nothing? NO!!! Nothing is better than this!!!!'

'...a ditch, an open sewer, Beirut under siege would get at least three stars compared to this – suggest you provide a Negative Star Rating System to accommodate the complete lack of service and downright hostility we were forced to endure.'

The rest Walt had to permanently erase due to bad taste, obscenity laws being what they are, even on the internet.

Yes, *the Drumhumble Inn* had to be seen for those reviews to be believed. Walt was almost convinced that this was *TikBox's* first series of 'sabotage reviews'. By a rival or rivals.

{He was correct but not for the reasons Walter Winston - or even Walter Mitty - could have imagined.}

3.

NO TREES

Walt should have known. He cursed. If you want to guarantee somebody, anybody, to appear, have a pee or a poo in the open air. Yeah, especially a crap and double especially when the last tree to go behind was last seen at least twenty miles back and more than 2 hours ago.

Two people on bikes, materialised out of the thin, now insufficient, mist. A large and small figure pedalling fast as if racing each other on the slight down incline of the single track. They were just about to pass his parked car. He saw one was a woman and suddenly wished he had gone further into the damp ankle high heather, far enough to allow the perversely rising mist to serve as a proper screen. But then he realised they could help him. He had certainly been seen. He had got their attention, yes, he had certainly got that. . .

The woman suddenly looked over at him then just as quickly averted her eyes, saying something sharp in an accent that Walt couldn't understand to the now giggling smaller figure who suddenly received a cuff to the back of the head. Hadn't Scotland outlawed smacking kids? It must have been something he or she said.

'Wait! Wait!' Walt shouted, his trousers now fully up but still unzipped, his shirt tails flapping in the rising wind hampering his stuffing them in as his fly caught in them and jammed.

They didn't stop or even slow but cycled on, faster.

'Can you please tell me the way to Drumhumble?!' Walt yelled as he reached the road again.

The small figure screamed something hellish and girlish. Walt watched as the smaller bike wobbled then crashed into the adjacent ditch.

The woman braked, dismounted, dropped her bike and bent to tend to what Walt now assumed to be a child – in all likelihood, her own.

Walt, now fully clothed and properly dressed did not know what to do.

The woman made up his mind. Quickly. Even from twenty or so metres away, despite the starting rain now speckling his specs, he could discern the rapid change in colours on the woman's face. From pallid white through pink, approaching crimson. She bent to remove what looked like an old-fashioned bicycle pump form her discarded bike. A big one. Both bike and pump and neither made of *bakelite*, both of heavy metal, and nothing to do with 'Lead' Zeppelin, Walt's serious panic was crazily punning in overdrive.

He caught about one word in about four as she screeched and stomped ever rapidly along the narrow road towards him, pump held high.

'Flashing…Sassenach and then *Child Abuse. . .ya English pervert!'*

He just made it back into the car, blessed the Mazda's sturdy glass as the pump battered against the driver's window.

He roared off, glancing and relieved to see the kid was now standing, snivelling and wiping tears away, sourly glaring and obviously shouting at Walt as he accelerated past.

He stopped at the summit of the next *brae* **(1)** got out and looked back. He was relieved to see the now tiny and tinier figures pedalling back in the opposite direction. Very slowly.

Back in the Mazda, he was about to set off when a thought hit him hard. A question really, forming, a worry mounting. . .was it his over-active imagination or was the kid's bike crash caused -- triggered – when he had used the word 'Drumhumble?'

4.

BAD SIGNS

If possible, Walt was more lost than ever. Another half hour or so had been added to his lostness. 30 minutes that had at least allowed his galloping heart thumps to come back down to somewhere near normal after narrowly escaping a pumping. Walt felt that was the only thing that was normal. By now he had, even excluding his toilet and near-violence break, been on this boring bloody track for what felt like for ever.

And still not a word from nippy *Nexus*. Still no signp. . . Walt never even got to 'post' in his caustic thinking.

There it was! As if by magic (and it was, but Walt could not know that. Then.).

    A signpost!

    And a crossroads.

    And the rain stopped. And the mist lifted. He felt it might be what his Scottish guide book had called 'haar'

Walt laughed, if only the sun would appear.

    And it did!

He briefly wondered if he should think of an unclothed female film star. . .

A shaft of strong sun light illuminated the signpost – the extremely narrow, almost laser-like beam appeared to be only on the well weathered wooden signpost. And nothing else.

The signpost did not have the normal crossroads four signs. There was nothing to indicate from where you had come – maybe Modern cliches like 'I know where you are coming from' were not allowed or more than likely still hadn't reached way up here, yet. Only three ancient wooden carved whiteish yellow arms: left, right, ahead pointed to each of three different tracks (even by Sahara desert norms they would never be classed as roads and if his ancient AA atlas had classed them it would be, at best, under F).

And all three pointers indicated the same destination:

DRUMHUMBLE.

He laughed. . .*Like the buses*, nothing for ages and all three appear at once. And all indicating his desired destination. . .But he thought about the blank: the unprovided one of the normally four direction posts – the one that should have pointed back in the direction he and the Mazda had come from. But it was only a fleeting thought. Too cursory. Too fleeting. A sign or lack of maybe. . .*no turning back*?

{Another mistake.}

He set off again, eventually choosing to take the direct route ahead ignoring both the left and right pointers.

{Another mistake. Two in fact.}

Walt's third mistake was to not look back once he had moved off because he would have seen the whole signpost revolve slowly through ninety degrees. Twice. Then again. Faster. Spinning.

A well-worn wooden Dervish.

CHAPTER 2: The State of Granny.

1.

The bugger of migraine.

GRANNY MULCH HAD a migraine. As a 749 year old sorceress, necromancer, wit/wiz-person, (she knew, even she, had to be careful with self-labelling these PC days) she could with her plethora of experience and myriad spells and umpteen tried -and- tested- on-normal mortals- potions, cure or fix most medical ails.

But migraine was a bugger.

This one was one of the worst.

Granny Mulch (aka GM) could not remember a time in all her years she was not plagued by migraines. The price you pay she felt for extra- extraordinary powers: extraordinarily severe migraines. But could she really rely on her memory? Maybe not recently, not this last fifty years – she guessed. She had to, as she couldn't remember. . .

She tried to concentrate again on that pesky signpost, trying to fix it. Stick it, secure it in its customary abnormal place. Lately it seemed to have a mind of its own or more likely a dose of the revolving fidgets. Hoaching **(1)** like mad; and It was vital now that it pointed in the directions GM dictated: normally the wrong directions. Usually for the singular purpose of *misdirection*.

But this time she wanted this current traveller to get through and to actually *find* and arrive safely in Drumhumble and not wander aimlessly lost and eventually give up trying to find her demesne. And her. She needed this Walter Wilson Winston. Urgently.

GM was painfully aware that small pool breeding bordering on in-breeding could only get you so far – the upside of meek and ignorant compliance of her villagers under total control was the danger of being swamped by the downside of idiocy.

Apart from Fergus there had been no new-borns or orphans abandoned in the glens for more than a century. Not like the good old days. So she needed a new strategy. Like kidnapping. . .without the ransom demands.

This Walter Wilson Winston (aka WWW.) Granny had checked up on. He had checked out. He seemed, *prima facie*, **(2)** a suitable candidate. She needed someone soon. Like right this minute if her gloomy predictions were correct. . . Someone like this WWW, GM hoped. An empirical, decidedly personal final in his face check would confirm this; once she had him *in situ* in her Drumhumble. Then Wally would be Granny's to do with as she pleased. If he passed her practical and physical muster as well as he had surmounted the honesty and conscientious hurdle she had posted in front of him with those deliberately awful reviews. She was pleased that he had bitten, that she was about to land him and forget all about those ghouls, trolls and nosey parkers that she had stirred up with her reviews and was forced to misdirect in their eventually fruitless attempts at visiting the Drumhumble Inn. *Her Drumhumble Inn*, the hub of *her* Drumhumble.

Her main reason for needing WWW. was to replenish the Drumhumble gene pool, but her more urgent need was to sort out Frugal McDougall. Her 'own wee Fergus' who was becoming too big for all the many boots with which she had provided him. Yes, she would see to it that Wally fitted both bills. Fix Frugal first then GM would Genetically Modify Drumhumble's breeding.

She got her head down, scrying again over her chipped basin of special water on her ancient kitchen (aka spell room) table. That infernal revolving signpost. . .

But a tsunami of intruding thoughts would not allow her to concentrate.

Hell's rotten wanwit teeth and buckets of rabid bat's blood, she could not help recalling the centuries of protection she had managed to afford Drumhumble all the wars and plagues and contraptions from which she had saved her village. . .she had created her unique *Scutum* for the God's sake!

But now she was struggling to fix a bloody signpost!

Migraines *were* a bugger.

This struggle was plainly and simply down to her endemic migraines, she rationalised. It could not be old age. . .

But like all rationalisations. . .even a witch's. . .

Granny Mulch was lying to herself.

2.

COL (SIC) de SAC

Another twenty minutes or so, at least – Walt had lost track of time, his digital watch had given up, gone as blank as his mobile phone and strangest of all the clock on the dashboard had disappeared as well. His hybrid laptop/tablet joined them too; it wouldn't even power up via the car battery and he was certain he had fully charged the laptop before setting of from, what now felt like, idyllic, flat, mildly interesting but decidedly *dry* Norfolk countryside.

Would his car and its battery fail him next? Was the car's blank clock the first sign. . . best not stop, just get out of here, wherever 'here' was, better to drive back and write the trip off to bad experience, over-ambition or to a too conscientious conscience. Or all three.

The State of Granny

That mountain, now right in front of him, staring down at him, right into his miserable face was a pretty definite clue that this track was going nowhere; it had in fact come to an end with a tight-knit rusted barbed wire mesh fence. Probably trying to dissuade 4x4 idiot drivers from tackling the slippery slope of the mountain. Not as high as a Munro, probably just a Graham, Walt reckoned, but formidable enough. There was no way round it in a car and he was certainly not abandoning the only electronic device he had that was still working. No, he was definitely keeping driving; just as long as the vital electrics in the Mazda didn't fail him like his other previous lifelines.

He drove off. In reverse.

Backing up, one arm around the seat back, straining neck and shoulders he reached the last passing place about two kilometres back. The alternative was risking stalling and not re-starting in the middle of a fifty-one-point turn that also risked ending up in a deep gurgling burn (they called them that up here) and he would *brook* no argument with the steep fall off on the other side. He didn't smile at his panicking punning.

Had the Scots never heard of *cul de sacs* (so much for the guidebook and their trumpeted *Auld Alliance*). Not even a Gaelic warning sign. *Neither Gallic nor Gaelic*, Walt grumped aloud.

He finally turned the car and accelerated a little, homeward bound.

At last, he reached that bloody signpost, half expecting to find it gone. But no, there it was, just visible, despite the haar that seemed to be bubbling and roiling around it. And nowhere else. He had a sudden vision of his O level teacher diclaiming some Shakespeae nonsense. . .The misty smokey whatever was only around it the post. It looked as if the Scots -- or was it Scotch? -- mist was trying to cloak the post and its faulty directions from view.

Then.

There was an almighty thunderclap and a split second later a flash of lightning that made Walt scream, slump down in his faux leather seat and clamp his eyes tightly shut, leaving him blind and shaking then wondering why the lightning/thunder order had been reversed. Lightning *then* thunder, but this had been *thunder preceding lightning*? Bizarre, or was that normal, Walt did his best with a scrambled mind and memory – but light was *supposed* to travel a lot faster than sound, wasn't it? But maybe it was normal for here – wherever *here* was.

He opened his right eye tentatively, then his left to gawp at a charred, smoking, signpost. Relieved that the Mazda and he had apparently escaped, he gingerly got out the car. He had to exit if he wanted to actually read the post. And he did. Now he could just make out that it had changed. . . altered.

    Considerably.

The cloud of smoke surrounding what remained of the signpost gradually dispersed. Walt nervously glanced between a still remarkably clear sky and the signpost. It now looked completely different.

 For one thing, there was only one 'thing'. That thing being the one arm that remained. And it pointed to:

DRUMHUMBLE

It pointed Right. And only right. No choice now. Apart from going back. . .

Maybe it was a sign. A sign from. . .God? Even.

The 'right' way, Maybe. At last. Walt couldn't help giggling and feeling a little chuffed as he drove and followed the sign ignoring its two smouldering erstwhile fallen 'branches' igniting the previously sodden surrounding now greedy bracken.

A recently 'rewilded' wolf or lynx's howl registered its disappointment at missing another meal...

3.

RIVER DREAD

Walt cheered up as he drove, his congenital optimism rose to full swing. Now he could blame the signpost and not his previous wrong choice. He, just then, never considered that he still had a choice: that of continuing as directed or back to Norfolk and his cosy flat. A flat he would soon be upgrading to an apartment more in keeping with the status he was approaching thanks to the mounting profits of his *Tikbox*. Warming with self-congratulations he wrapped more delicious thoughts around him. Yes, once that next Biggie of a contract was a done deal with the UK's third Biggest Hotel Chain.. ..all those clicks on *his TikBox* site.. ..all those bookings for the hotel rooms.. ..all the commissions to Walt Wilson Winston, WWW, *The* www.Entrepreneur...

Walt's mind was on the Bigger Road ahead but his eyes were not on the immediate track in front as he dreamed on, oblivious to it narrowing further, the rain now sweeping down and across from the receding mountain on his left. The windscreen wipers, rather than alerting him to the deteriorating driving conditions, were providing an accompanying soundtrack, a soporific rhythm to his dreams, now accompanied by the four wheels seemingly rumbling, *Drumhumble, Drumhumble, Drumhumble...*

At essence Walter Wilson was an optimist. His glass was never half empty, mostly it was beyond half full, chiefly brimming, brimming over, often with over confidence, despite the painful past performances and what to most others would have been dispiriting and debilitating experiences, often complete disasters.

But all that *merde* was behind him, in the past, chucked in the Big Dustbin for shelf stacking; checking out; serving rude drinkers; permanent night shift floor polishing etc etc et- boring- demeaning-cetera.

Walt was in the middle of slowly removing Uma Thurman's granddaughter's diaphanous chemise – she had been clothed for all of thirty seconds, the eternity that had passed since she had brazenly knocked on the door of his new luxury penthouse -- when he hit the wall.

Literally.

It wasn't a conventional wall of brick and mortar or even breeze block but it had acted as just as effectively. It was something Walt could not see but it had been solid enough to batter the Mazda and Walt sideways, spinning them round and round then down a long steep slippery slope of scree, now hurtling him headlong into a slow flowing river.

4.

GM, RESCUES WWW

Why does keech (aka shite) always come in bunches? GM (aka Granny Mulch) cursed. First the migraine, now several degrees worse, then, the recalcitrant signpost, now her damned Portal – left it shut hadn't she? The whole Shield (aka *Scutum*) shut. Closed. Impenetrable. And Wally and his infernal bloody stupid wee combustion-engined, environment-polluting sports car had run smack into it.

Jesus Joseph Mary Martin Luther Johns Calvin and Knox plus the Pope in a Basket, how could she forget to open it for him? Forget?! She was a witch for Buddha's sake. . .

GM knew it wasn't just the migraine. Not purely the insistent persistent throbbing pain and jumping, now galloping flashing spots before her eyes. Oh aye, they didn't help her concentration, her mind, her powers. . .where was she. . .oh aye.

No, it was her age. There had been signs recently that she was losing it. . .fast. Too fast. She was determined to see her 750th birthday. She had been planning the BIG Party since her 700th in 2000. . . But. . . even all bad things come to an end; *reverse entropy,* she wondered. Any way you looked at it, the recent evidence, ever since that damned millennium, she knew she was at more than a watershed in her too short life.

GM felt she was past her Spell-By Date

But despite the migraine clamping her temples and banging on her brow she focussed on rescuing this Wally from the bed of the River Dread. Yet another normal mortal she would have to save since the invention of the infernal combustion engine, when they insisted on trying to drive, find, invade and contaminate Drumhumble.

Her Drumhumble.

But this Wally she had to save and *had to* let Inside. She had researched him and she intuited he was her solution to the mounting problem with Frugal. Her Fergus. Frugal McDougall, foundling, found by GM on her doorstep on the eve of her 700th birthday party. So that made Frugal. . . turned fifty. . .

Eureka and Gadzooks! That was the cause of his problem, causing his itchy feet, his discontent his. . . Male Menopause! *Belated* Male Menopause. Maybe he would settle for a motor bike or a sports car. . .no, that was stupidly daft -- no car had ever been driven in her Drumhumble -- over her dead body -- but it brought her bursting brain back to the Mazda that Wally was drowning in.

If only she had remembered to read the *Post It* stickers she had on her wee portable fridge:

'Clear the River Dread of old wrecks'.

She might well have read the self-reminders. If she could remember where she had put the fridge.

5.

TOO HOT TO HANDLE

Walt came to and tried to splutter.

He was underwater! The Mazda was filling rapidly. Despite his panic – so Big that he couldn't think of any apposite puns- he remembered what to do. He had seen enough movies to tell him to wait until the water level reached the interior car roof and hold his breath, then open the door when the pressures outside and inside had equalised . . .or something. . .and swim to safety. Or something. . .?

Bugger that for a game of submariners! He grabbed the door handle and screamed – well tried to. The water had reached his mouth. It tasted foul, like an Islay malt without the alcohol, all horrible peat and now impossible to spit out.

The door handle!

It was red hot! Actual sparks shot out of it now, sizzling into the water. Would he be electrocuted *and* drowned?

6.

A CAT, A BIRD, A WITCH (but no Wardrobe)

'Let *me* open the phequing thing for you, ya wally!' GM was beginning to wonder if her research had let her down. Was this Wally suitable for breeding purposes? She was desperate for the introduction of new blood, and maybe Frugal just needed a break. . . but maybe not this desperate. . .maybe she should let this Wally drown? Okay he seemed honest and conscientious but these assets were as nothing if he was as glaikit **(3)** as this.

Her research had told her nobody would miss him, the Wally, this archetypal loner, no friends, no colleagues and no family. An only lonely child who last year lost his parents in a car crash. . . maybe he should just 'go' that way too? GM was into symmetry and irony – preferably an admixture of both, yes, let him lie in the River Dread's bed? Along with all the ancient wrecks. A suitable resting place for all ghastly cars and their drivers.

But GM was not only made of sterner stuff but also of (slightly) compassionate material. She hadn't really given Wally a chance, had she? And she was nearly sure she needed him. The wonky signpost was definitely her fault. And The Scutum had been doing its normal Total Security job. It was *her* job to open it when necessary. Only she could. If only she had remembered. . .again the fault was hers.

Yes, give the boy a chance. One more anyway. . .

Maybe he wasn't a wally but truly a Walt or even a Sir Walter, turning out to be the knight she needed before she slipped unprotestingly into that Dark Night that she felt was too close. . .yes. . . a real knight like one of her many great heroes. (Well, you are bound to have *some* after 749 years). Sir Walter Raleigh. . .GM reached for her clay pipe and quickly filled it with Sir Walter's wonderful discovery **(4)** and import. . . Her one proper vice these days. Tobacco: Variety- *Golden Drumhumble* **(5),** locally grown and cured to perfection.

Troubled no end, she spoke aloud: 'This is at least a "one pipe problem"'.

'No shit, Sherlock! No shit-' squawked Cocky her Cockatoo.

'- Not funny.' Her cat and familiar, Toby, interrupted, purred and demurred.

'Shut up the pair of you! Bluidy migraine's bad enough without you two starting.'

7.

DE-HYDRATED

Suddenly the driver's door flew open. How the hell. . ? Walt did not take the time to finish wondering. He frantically side stroked out the car and into the river that had by now filled his car with its dark-brown gurgling water.

On the way to the surface, Walt the car buff (he was getting a state-of- the- art Mercedes next he dreamed, part of his Five Year Plan) tangled with – in no particular order, as they say-

A *Triumph Herald*

A *Sunbeam Alpine*

A gangster style 1930s *Buick*

And what must have been one of Henry Ford's model Ts off that first assembly line and lastly a *Hillman Imp. Best place for it,* the car buff in Walt couldn't help but think.

The State of Granny

But no skeletons, and no bodies and most importantly not his.

Walt scrambled, crawled, clawed and slithered his way back up the steep slope, the crumbling shifting scree reluctantly yielding a slow exhausting sodden climb.

He chittered, shivered and dripped on the sodden dirt road, now more a mud track as he looked back down to the peat-blackened river. It appeared from this height to be really fast flowing now. Faster anyway. He realised the rain was pouring. The teeming cataract making little difference to his wetness apart from making his eyes sting, making his glasses. . .his frantic grope told him his specs were in the river. . .along with his car, his smart phone, his laptop -- all his lifelines, including his spare pair of specs.

The adrenaline released by his escaping vanished under a rising incoming wave: a tsunami of panic. And no concomitant puns.

Death by drowning might soon be replaced by hypothermia.

He screwed up his wet, quasi-myopic eyes and surveyed as much as he could see in the downpour. Nothing but moor, a few rocks and the odd tuft of fully flowering heather that was well past its blooming date in late October.

Isolation. Desolation. Despair. And blooming heather.

Feeling completely naked in his sodden 'thinly striped' navy blue and white 'business shirt' (now 'see-through'), charcoal grey suit trousers, black dress shoe and black socks, he would have traded all his sodden gear for any one of. . .his car -- with a working Sat Nav, his mobile phone or his lap top. . . and of course a connection to The Net. . .plus his left behind drowned shoe. . .

He had not a clue as to what to do next but decided he might as well have one question answered before he snuffed it.

What the hell was it --the Invisible Wall -- that had thrown the Mazda and him off the puddled dirt track he was now standing on? He could see nothing, but despite the river trauma he definitely remembered hitting SOMETHING.

8.

BIRD, CAT & WITCH

Hope for the boy yet? GM was still ambivalent about that. So, Walter, despite his ordeal, was still *curious*. She *thought* she liked that. She would see.

Cocky the cockatoo chirped up *'Only human, only human. Nature not Nurture. Nature Not Nurture.'*

GM ignored the cheeky bird.

But Toby the cat didn't. If Cocky said 'sugar', Toby was bound to say 'shite'. Always Voices-*Versa*, so now Toby meowed loudly, condescendingly:

'Rubbish! Studies prove Nurture predominates and Curiosity-'

"Killed the cat!' GM bawled. She could only stand so much.

Cocky began to cackle. A pale imitation of a witch's version but a cackle nonetheless. And much more annoying.

'And I'll be opening that cage door my girl and introducing you -- up front, in your face and personal to Toby here. He's been eyeing you for all of your 14 short years. And may the best animal win. Then I MIGHT GET SOME PEACE!'

GM lit up again, puffed furiously, ignoring the coughs and muted protests from the creatures subjected to passive smoking and all its putatively horrible effects.

'C'mon Wally boy' she said as she lowered her head again to the ancient table, the scars and stains upon which could tell many a story.

Tales to have you spellbound.

Literally.

9.

THE THING (aka IT) (aka The Shield) (aka the *Scutum*)

Walt was sure it was here. This must be the very spot where he and the Mazda had hit. . .and he hit IT again. With his forehead this time. He had walked right into IT.

He rose groggily, feeling for damage, relieved that there was no blood on his fingers, but a swelling was rapidly. . .well swelling. God, it felt it the size of a grape, now a plum, would it be melon-size next? And his nose was bigger too – he regretted all those vain posturings in the mirror and his wish list that included anything to replace his too- tiny retroussé conk.

But as suddenly as they had grown, the contusions shrivelled and disappeared.

Walt slowly, with both hands outstretched before him, again approached IT. The invisible IT. His right hand ever so gingerly finally made contact. He was touching IT. Feeling IT and now feeling a tingle from its smoothness, expecting that to grow into a full blown, fully charged electric shock, but he bravely kept his hand there, the sensation so pleasing -- like the hand warmer he used for winter pitch and putt -- that he placed both hands on IT.

God, it felt good.

He peered. Trying to see through IT. Despite the obscuring rain and his weak eyes he was convinced that just through IT the sun was shining. The sun! Shining!

IT was a watershed. A literal watershed by the opaque looks of it.

Gradually Walt felt IT in all directions. Up as far as he could reach; down to road level; IT extended beyond the narrow road and into the ditch; now the moor and heather as he side-stepped like a crabbed-gaited sleepwalker with both hands rigidly in front, feeling. And fearing. Afraid that there was no end to IT, no way through IT.

And the only course of action was to return the way he came. All the way back to Norfolk.

10.

MEDIEVAL IMPRECATIONS.

GM cursed and cursed, using words unheard of for hundreds of years. Neither the young Cocky, nor the middle-aged (by familiar measures) Toby had ever heard Granny talk like this. The odd 'verily' and 'zounds and *Beelzeebub, Mephistopholes and Nicolo Machiavelli* but these other, obviously archaic phrases -- interspersed with more familiar Anglo Saxon – were mostly lost upon cat and bird.

Unless these queer words were part of a New Spell? Maybe against them both, bird and cat, if they were not more careful. They eyed each other, in a rare *silent,* scared-induced harmony.

'Phloost!. . .Rydeenabing. . .astaferikyst!' GM knew she was losing it. . . A Big Emergency and she overlooks the simple fact that Walter cannot enter her village without her opening the one Portal in The Shield.

And she *forgets!*

C'mon! Focus, Nikki. . .' GM was slevvering now, the silver strands of saliva slowly dangling, slipping, plopping down onto the ancient kitchen table as she tried her best to allow Walter Wilson Winston into her world, despite the migraine, her apparently waning powers, not forgetting her faulty memory. . . . if she could.

11.

A FOSBURY FLOP (nearly)

Walt was convinced the way ahead was completely blocked. IT was. . .well an invisible all around, wraparound IT. And through his adjusting vision he could now make out that damned tantalising sun on the other side of IT. Something beyond strange was going on. With himself too. Or was it just the bright sunlight that was fooling him into thinking his eyesight had all of a sudden improved?

Maybe he had drowned after all? Perhaps this was a modern Purgatory? Or a variation on the eternally damned lot of Tantalus? Cold and freezing with a warming, healing sun just out of touch? Unreachable.

He knew that there was nothing for it but the long road back to civilisation -- or what passed for it in this God forsaken, wet and dreary landscape; probably death in some form of hypothermia would hit him first. The warmth from IT to his hands had gone no further. The rest of him was chilled. And shivering. Now trembling,

Cold plus Fear equals Misery.

He was sure he had read that hypothermia wasn't the worst way to go. You gently fall into a Blessed Sleep didn't you. . .?

He retraced his muddy steps, almost made it back to where he had started, where IT had hit his Mazda, or rather vice versa as the Mazda was moving and IT apparently didn't; he was certain now that as far as he was concerned this IT went on *for ever* in every direction. If this was really a Reality.

Climbing the ditch back at the roadside, with his foot on the far edge of the bank, the turf gave way and he slipped, then twisted and in trying to regain his balance he fell backwards, certain that he would bang his head again, against IT. . .the back of his head *for a change* he instantly consoled himself using his last vestige of optimism.

But instead, he fell IN.

And was suddenly bathed in sunshine. His clothes already rapidly heating to steamed dry.

A soughing whisper just behind him made him reach back to touch IT. This time he did get a real shock. Whatever it was that had gained him access appeared to have vanished. . .or more likely, *closed*.

But he was IN.

{But would he ever get OUT?}

12.

WITCH'S WARNING

'Gotcha!' GM gave her happy version of a 749 year old (and feeling it) witch's cackle then fell forward, just missing her basin of scrying water but hitting her head on her big kitchen table. She remained there. Still.

'*She dead! She dead!*' Cocky accompanied his Caribbean-accented squawk (one of the best in his mimicry repertoire) with a fluttering of wings, his white crest ruffling the top of his large (for a budgie) cage as he fluttered up and down.

'*Shut up you stupid bird.*' One of the few things Toby, the black cat, GM's favourite familiar, couldn't do, well wouldn't do, was, panic.

Cats, especially familiars, are cool. Cool cats, dopey dogs and brainless birds.

Toby stretched from his cosy cushion on the Big Chair, the one nearest the peat-log burner, and slowly slunk over to look up at the slumped form of his mistress.

Toby had to admit it didn't look good. No sign of life. Time for, if not desperate or drastic, at least, radical measures. Toby had lived long enough to know that even *familiar* cats with their 19 lives had to adapt to survive. This is *a time to adapt, Toby*, he told himself and nimbly leaped up on to the kitchen table.

Toby slowly put out his tongue.

'Psshaw!! GM awoke. 'Get off me you messy cat. What are you. . .? You think you're a dirty dog?! Licking a *human's* face?! You'll be asking me to take you for an aimless *walk* next!' AND GET OFF MY TABLE!! How many times do I have to tell you?!'

Cocky's *schadenfreude* knew no bounds. Vicious birds and unempathetic people have an abundance of that stuff only the Germans could nail down with their ugly sounding (but concise, precise) language.

Cocky ran up and down the ladder in her cage ringing the wee bell at the top every time, as if keeping some sort of score that she would finally annoy that cat with at every opportunity.

Toby imagined the unadulterated glee saturating every off-white feather.

'But you are not a *human-*' a hurt Toby began.

'No, I am a witch. And you are a pedant.'

'But I, thought. . .*we* thought-"Toby faltered, he should have known better than to look for support from The Bird.

The Granny State of Drumhumble

'Bloody rubbish. Bloody rubbish. Never did. Never did. Not me. Not-'

'What thought? Thought what?!' GM screeched a fair imitation of a 14 year old Australian cockatoo. But she looked at Toby.

'*Nothing.*' Toby now back in the Big Chair curling up, just resisted the temptation to say that a 749 year old witch should *know* what even a clever cat and certainly a bird-brained cockatoo was thinking.

And she did. Of course. Eventually. . . She was Granny Mulch after all.

'Wee bit tired. That's all. Been a brute of a day. . .' GM mumbled to herself knowing it was about to get, if not worse, then a damned sight busier.

'Right, you two. Best behaviour. We are going to have a *visitor*-'

'Hate visitors. Hate-'

'*Who?*' Toby quick-purred to stop that Blasted Bird; a familiar just knew when propitiation was most appropriate, compulsory even, if a familiar was to keep its job. And its life. The 17th. He fully intended attending his centenary celebration and opening his telegram from his Queen Nikki.

'I need peace and quiet. I have important business to discuss with my Fergus, Fergus McDougall. *Mister* McDougall to you two.'

'Not him. Not him. Hate him. Really hate-'

'Shut up!' Witch and cat shouted and miaowed (loudly) in concert again.

GM stood and strode quickly (for a 749 year old) to grab Cocky the cockatoo's cage cover from underneath the cage and swiftly wrapped the 'Silencer' that was also known as GM's 'Comforter' in times of stress. Times like these. Toby got little time to enjoy his feline schadenfreude as GM barked:

The State of Granny

'And you, get off the Big Chair. You know it's reserved for VISITORS!'

CHAPTER 3: FRUGAL McDOUGAL.

1.

THE MAN HIMSELF

FRUGAL (AKA FERGUS) McDougal, innkeeper, brewer, ex- postmaster, funeral wake director, golf professional, amateur dentist, justice of the peace, procurator fiscal, judge, jury, entrepreneur and anything else that Granny deemed apposite to cram into his burgeoning portfolio was increasingly fed up with his many lots. Especially these last long dog days of this late October summer.

He decided to take a stroll. First thing in the morning. He did not want to meet anyone and have to put a face on things. That would be the first for ages. Frugal had only two faces due to his lifelong hypomania: Menacing or Mild depending on which of the two poles he presently inhabited. Currently he was a raging polar bear and definitely not a cute penguin. Overall, he was the walking talking, spitting, shouting epitome of the Caledonian Dichotomy. . .albeit with a weighting heavily biased towards Mr Hyde rather than Dr Jekyll.

He left 'his' Drumhumble Inn and turned towards the east looking for some inspiration and a lot of determination from the sun that was just keeking around the taller peak of Ben Her. **(1)**

Frugal was fed up, yes, but right now even more unhappy, one hundred per cent scunnered. **(2)** and not a little perturbed that the time had come to face up, fifty year old man up, to Granny Mulch. His foster mother. He knew the confrontation would be painful. For them both.

Nearly fifty years, boy and man (as far as he knew and if Granny Mulch was telling the whole truth -for once) *and never a step beyond this place,* he steeled himself.

But Frugal McDougal did not kid himself that this was the root cause of his scunneration , not the real cause of his current agitation and angst, not just the too-full days and nights that now just seemed to go on and on and had become unbearable.

No, it was the Big Issue that he had to confront Granny with. He would couch it in the shape of a present for himself for his alleged fiftieth birthday.

More and more, the older he got, he wondered where he had come from and who his real mother was who had abandoned him on Granny's back step, apparently during the celebration for Granny's 700th birthday. He wondered if his mother was alive. Maybe he could find her. Maybe even his father. . .?

Yes, enough was enough. More than. Frugal felt he had done more than enough to pay Granny back for. . .well everything. . .and then some. Yes, he had more than earned a break. What was it called again? Oh yes. . .something he had never had. . .

A holiday.

Outside.

Outside and anywhere. . .anywhere but Drumhumble.

2.

WALT IN WONDERLAND

Walt felt wonderful. He wondered when he had last experienced this oceanic feeling. Never. He was lying on his back on the ditch bank staring at a lapis lazuli sky. He was dry, warm, comfortable. A gentle, friendly sun shone down on Walter Wilson Winston, the www. Entrepreneur ('extraordinary' pending appending).

He wished he could lie here for EVER. Right at this moment all thoughts of his burgeoning online business, all rampant ambitions. . . everything, even previously persistent cloying worries about having never had a girlfriend was banished. Everything gone, past and future, nothing but the Here and the Now. . .Bliss.

Walt was falling asleep and began trying to dream of sex. This was the nearest he had been to sex with someone, anyone (else) in 25 years. 'In your dreams!' as they say. He tried hard to conjure up himself with Uma Thurman 111 or Naomi Watts 1V, then the three of them together in a huge polythene bag filled with scented masseuse's oil (the oil not the masseuse. . .on second thoughts. . .they chased each other around the bag trying to grab a hold of the nearest body part. . . but he had to settle for Natalie Portman11. Old Natalie again. And on her own. What was it about Natalie these last few dreams? She was more and more taking over what passed for Walt's Love Life. . .still, that skimpy white leather gear looked promising. . .and *the appurtenance* in her right hand. . .

3.

GRANNY KENS YE KEN

Frugal (aka as Fergus) had intended walking towards the sun for as long as it took to prepare his spiel to Granny but he never reached the east end of Drumhumble's one long narrow street. He was well short of the last thatch- roofed cottage when he felt it.

He should have known it would come.

It tugged him across the silent road, through Grandpa Clarke's Wynd, past the blacksmith's yet unopened smiddy and up the incline of the overgrown lane, the wild brambles, briars and angrier rambling roses pricking, scolding him for his naivety.

He should have known. He had experienced it, over the umpteen years as Granny's lieutenant in Drumhumble. Her right and only hand man since he took over the running of the Inn from Harmless Henderson. Harmless -- the last mug to run the show for GM. To run *her* show. But Harmless had died.

At exactly 75 years of age. Like everybody else. On their birthday.

Precisely.

Well Frugal McDougal was not for staying in harness then snuffing it still under Granny's yoke like poor auld gormless Harmless.

But why did he, Frugal McDougal, think for one moment that Granny would *not* just *know* what he was thinking of asking? Right now, this very minute, she would know he was *planning* to ask for that birthday present: that was not the best of preparations. None at all. Just the opposite, annoying 'his' Granny by *trying* to keep his thoughts to himself.

Yes, Granny Mulch was 'calling'. Calling 'her boy' to call.

Now!

4.

MAYBE IN KANSAS

A pleasant zephyr coaxed Walt awake again. He stretched, stood up, then suddenly remembered his ordeal escaping from his Mazda in that black river. . .the weird business with the, whatever IT was, that had suddenly aloowed him in. In. To. What?

He looked around. Then turned back. Despite himself, he felt for, what he now thought of as, The Opening. He found IT. But not The Opening. He spun a few times checking, still looking in wonder but now declining the sharp shock that each previous tentative touch had yielded. No way back. But WHERE was he now?

Was he in Oz?!

The contrast from dreary *Kodachrome* to glorious technicolour in the Wizard of Oz (he watched the film every Xmas) immediately hit him. Back from where he had come –'Outside' -- as far as he could see was 'in' black and white and still raining. Miserable. *Dreich,(3)* Walt remembered that was number one in a list of the *Top Ten Peculiar Particularly Onomatopoeic Scottish Words.*

But, in 'Here', inside IT, everything was in glorious sun lit *colour*. But unlike in Oz, this *could be* Kansas. Kansas in colour! Ripe fields of various lush head high brown and yellow crops lined both sides of the dirt track. From the little he could see by jumping up, only small sections were apparently harvested.

In the Highlands of Scotland? In late October?!

Walt had no decision to make. Back was out. Forward was the only thing for it, well, apart from lying down in that cosy grass verge. For the rest of his life. But this glorious sun could not last for ever. In the Highlands, c'mon? he laughed. Even in *these* peculiarly exotic Highlands. Euphoric or not, he would surely eventually need shelter. And fed. And watered. . .

Walt was suddenly ravenous. And thirsty. Maybe he should have swallowed some of that river after all. Maybe he had and that had added to his thirst and perhaps he should risk exploring the unknown crops for some instant food?

Despite the dirt track not being built of yellow brick Walt was sure that it was the way ahead, the only one to follow. The only way. He whistled '*We're off to see the wizard*' now as he walked, somehow certain that there would be a sign that would not be purely metaphorical but literal and preferably 'fixed' in its signalling – *aye laddie,* (he was practising the language), he would settle for 'fixed'.

Walt was wrong. No sign. Yet.

Now he felt tired, despite what he felt had been a long and sound sleep, and he was thirstier and hungrier. This felt a bit like that walking holiday he had taken in Devon with the hedgerows so high that nothing else was visible. This time it was with amazingly abundant, golden, most often strange crops. A few he thought he recognised. Maybe barley and wheat, but more than twice as many again he had no idea what they were. Despite being from bucolic Norfolk he had never taken an interest in 'country things': computers and all associated 'stuff -- all *indoors* -- had been Walter Wilson Winston's total leisure activity outside school. And inside it too. Until he started Tik Box.

In the distance he could now just see a mountain with two rounded peaks that somehow appeared as if it was about to lose both its snowy toppings -- probably Global Warming in this bizarre Highland Heat. Walt wished it was closer. Then he could maybe climb a foothill and gain a view of where he was; give him an idea, some perspective; most importantly gauge where he was going, where he could go and must travel for water and food. And eventual shelter before nightfall.

5.

NONE SO BLIND.

Walt's tired legs knew that for the last half kilometre or so he had been gently climbing. He wondered if maybe past rain had obliterated any sign of life ever using this track- human, animals or vehicle but the light brown dirt that he scuffed now with his dusty, now dry, shoe and sock still yielded no sign but little crumbs of earth and puffs of choking dust. Strange that his shoeless foot experienced no pain on the hard track. A *sock absorber,* walt giggled. . .

At last, the knackering climb came to an end. As did the head high lush crops that were now behind him waving farewell in the cooling breeze as he gratefully began a steeper downward path. Then stopped. Jaw dropped. Gob smacked. Shocked and delighted. . .

Civilisation!

Not that far, at the end of the ever-downward slope, a couple of kilometres at most, was a long narrow row of houses. His relief mounted in concert with his increased energy temporarily holding at bay his thirst and hunger.

Despite his apparently miraculous cure for his erstwhile myopia, Walt's spurt of elation blinkered him from the sight of the adjacent foliage of the vines: the inchoate pale pink grapes clearly visible to anyone who glanced sideways. Nor did he take in that the smoke from one of the nearing houses was, even at this distance, a vivid green.

6.

ON THE THRESHOLD

Frugal stood on the doorstep – allegedly the same one upon which he had been dumped as a *babby*, just a few hours old -- according to Granny.

He tentatively reached for the huge wrought iron door knocker that as a boy he often expected its weight and normal use would see an end to the ancient age- blackened oak door.

It would be far from the first time the mammoth knocker had given him a violent electrical shock, enough once to knock him off his feet when he was just out of short trousers but still being 'naughty'. A few times it was neither pure mischief nor malice, purely the collateral damage from a witch's daily exercises, practising her dark esoteric craft.

Most often though, the shock was utilitarian: a warning that Granny was not to be disturbed. Not this time apparently. Granny was expecting him. Commanding his presence.

Before Frugal could wrap with the heavy knocker the door opened. Her voice called:

'Enter, my boy.'

7.

LOCAL GREETINGS

Walt reached what might loosely be described as a pavement beside what might even more loosely be termed the Main Street of this village; apparently the only street but it stretched away gently inclining upwards to the horizon and the still rising sun. The gimcrack road, on both sides, was hemmed with squashed terraced cottages, each roof thatched in what looked like pristine yellow straw that was gilded by the sun that slowly began to bathe all of the village.

He noticed for the first time the vertical vivid green spirals of smoke from a chimney a little back from this street.

Walt, the film buff of classic Hollywood movies could not help a flash, not of Oz now, but of *Brigadoon*. Maybe the sun was the cue for village life to emerge – daily hopefully rather than every 100 years. . .

Walt's film fuelled imagination segued to Westerns. Classic cowboys. . . The pavement and road being unpaved, Walt half expected desultory tumbleweeds to make a rolling entrance any minute and continue through the emptiness. He nearly turned to check for an out - of - control stagecoach replete with a terrified driver and a shotgun companion gasping his last about the sixth Native American arrow that. . .but his enchanting fantasy was interrupted by his first signs of human life.

With no measure of the time but guessing by the sun -- if it was really still October it must be around ten o' clock, if it was Norfolk, but up here. . .?

Walt watched three children materialise from a doorway some few houses ahead. With hessian satchels on their backs they began their approach on the same side of the 'street' he walked.

Walt guessed they were siblings, their height and shape suggesting a couple of years in respective age differences. Each wore a taupe coloured smock that reached to their knees. They were bare legged and the tallest was bare footed, the other two wearing what appeared to be clogs. They were getting closer but so far seemed unaware of Walt, too engrossed in what looked like a violent version of 'Tig'.

'Good Morning-', Walt began, but before he could ask about the availability of drink and food in their village, the three instantly stopped their frantic pushing and pulling game, took Walt in then rapidly scuttled across to the other side of the 'street' and hurried on.

>Walt turned, looked back at them.

>All three stopped and turned back too.

He could see the fear, terror even, on the kids' faces. All three. Worrying, he continued further into the otherwise deserted village.

Suddenly a front door of the next cottage in the terrace on his side opened and a large woman in a voluminous olive-green pinafore came out. She held a chipped enamel cream and blue pail in one hand and a cloth in the other.

The big woman dropped the pail on seeing Walt now almost alongside her. The abandoned pail's water sloshed over Walt's one shoe and both socks as she screamed and slammed her door shut.

He passed her closed door and for some murky reason half expected her to re-emerge brandishing, of all things, a big black bicycle pump.

Walt squelched on to come upon two women exiting a cottage chatting earnestly with each other. They were on the opposite side.

'Good morning, ladies,' Walt expected them to bolt indoors as he quickly continued 'I don't suppose you know of somewhere I could buy a drink and something to. . .eat.' His voice trailed off in the face of the hostile glares and the arms-folded chilling silence that defied any colloquy.

He shivered and slunk onwards along the long, terraced row, too aware of the almost palpable menace from behind. He expected he would reach the end of this pavement before. . .

But. . .there it was. His destination. He vaguely remembered it. The name triggered it.

He had arrived.

The Drumhumble Inn.

8.

INN YE COME

No-one could accuse the Drumhumble Inn's façade of resembling a portal to Shangri La but to Walter Wilson Winston it seemed at that moment to promise much more: Salvation.

Walt had almost walked past it. The Inn was congruous with all the other terraced dwellings but with a treble frontage. It must be centuries old Walt figured, with an authentic look most of Norfolk hostelries craved but would never for hundreds of years match.

He scoured the frontage. The one sign, *'Drumhumble Inn'*, in fading wood-carved script above the solid front door was the only sign. No mention of food, not even drink. But there must be. . .surely. But, judging by his earlier receptions in Drumhumble, he was prepared for there to be 'no room at the inn', nor food nor drink. . .

Walt tried the door.

He lost his bet with himself. It was unlocked. He pushed then shoved it open trying to enter. Despite multitude creaks and groans – mostly from the recalcitrant door -- Walt got inside.

He forgot to congratulate himself on 'reaching his destination' as his Sat Nav would have done if *Nexus* had not been drowned in the Mazda but at present he had no recollection of that 'accident', let alone *Nexus* or *Mazda*. . .

(And later he would come to learn that *Nexus*'s suggested route from Inverness to Drumhumble had been sabotaged. . .by, who else. . but Granny Mulch.)

CHAPTER 4: ONE-SIDED NEGOTIATIONS

1.

NO CONTEST

FRUGAL KNEW GM meant business. There was no sign of that infernal cat, Toby. As a boy he had stupidly fought Toby for Granny's affection, most often losing.

The cat would still, no doubt, despite its age, be out on the ran dan, wishing there was tiles instead of the ubiquitous thatch to have 'a night on.' Toby still gave Frugal the creeps. More than Granny even. He knew that the cat was an extension, kind of, of its owner: the evil side of Granny, he was sure.

But more significantly the infuriating cockatoo, Cocky, had been shut up, in the shrouded cage.

'Well, Fergus, long time no see-eth. Verily. Too long I would say.' Granny gave him her knowing smile. All knowing. 'I know how busy you are but a wee social call to your dear auld Granny now and then would not be amiss – I take it that this visit is *not* of that ilk.'

Fergus's half-prepared spiel, his whole case, dissolved in the face of Granny's all too knowing smile.

'I know that you know that I know that you-' Frugal stumbled. Stumbling, almost stuttering now *blushing*. . .at nearly fifty, he swatted away the horrible thought of possible witnesses. *Get a grip, McDougal*. . .

'Come, come, Fergus. Why so nervous? It's only Granny, just thee and me. Me and my indispensable full time right- hand factotum, amanuensis and occasional confidante, who ever so capably administers *all* Drumhumble. . . 'things' -- for want of a better generic?'

Frugal should have expected this. As ever, a catchweight contest, no contest really: Granny Mulch v Frugal McDougal the result? In the first minute, the first few seconds – one *knock* and *out*.

'Is this the *man* who has the entire community at his beck and call, the *man* who rules the roost, the *man* who has everyone in awe and fearful of him, the king of the castle, the *man* who Thomas Hobbes would have lauded until he snuffed it in his nineties musing in Malmesbury. Oh, how old Tommy H would have loved you Fergus McDougal. The epitome of the absolute monarch he was proposing to solve the philosophical problem of what do with individual freedom in the potential anarchy in the aftermath of his *English* civil war.'

As usual Granny lost him in her archaic and esoteric references, but unusually she was. . .well it was almost as if she was making his case for him.

Of course she was! Spiking his guns, taking the wind out of his sails and *clipping his wings*; stopping him flying, fleeing *her* coop, nest, roost, domain, demesne, realm, empire. He almost resigned himself to hearing her out, worrying what was *her plan* was *for him* but knowing her dark powers from close experience for too long he had to. . .to. . .must stop her or at least deflect her. Somehow.

He should have known she had a plan. A plan for him, 'her Fergus'. And so much better thought through than his pathetic attempt that was both, Dross and Gross. . .

He heard himself blurt:

'A holiday! A birthday present. . .a special birthday!'

In the silence that grew, Frugal was briefly tempted to rip the cloth off of the bird cage and shelter in the inevitable diverting repetitive inanities of the cockatoo. That would have been better than the silence surrounding the malevolent grin that formed on Granny's withered face.

Anything would have been better.

Anything.

2.

WALT IN THE INN

Walt was just inside the ancient front door. Through the musty gloom he watched the back of a bent figure who was gently wafting a broom across the uneven grey stone floor. Walt was surprised that the creaking racket that he made in his struggle to get the door open hadn't warned the sweeper of his presence. Maybe it was the loud singing and desultory humming in time to the lazy movements of his broom. The tunes were unfamiliar but definitely Country and Western: an apparent medley of snippets as if the singing sweeper were memorising a set from a repertoire. All pitched perfectly in a high register.

'Excuse me.' Walt tried again 'Excuse me! Still nothing. If anything, the singing was louder, the odd discernible words interspersed with loud hums.

'My son calls another man daddy

Dum dum dum dum his name or his face.'

Why do you run and hide from life

Dum de dum just aint smart…

The sweeping abruptly upped in time with the next tune's tempo…

Jambolayo, crawfish pie dumdem…'

Walt tentatively approached the back of the figure, whom he reckoned was indeed a man. Probably an old man given the bent posture and weak movements.

Walt gently tapped the back of the shoulder of the cracked grey leather waistcoat.

'Aaah!' The old man jumped and turned shouting something incomprehensible. Probably in Gaelic.

They faced each other but both began backing away. Both obviously scared. One smelling. Awful. And getting worse rapidly.

'Sorry. Sorry. I didn't mean to frighten you, it's just that. . .well I am in need of drink. . .and food. Yes, I am thirsty, parched actually. And a bit hungry. Starving. . . if truth be known.'

The old man's eyes widened further. His wispy white and yellow hair was starting to rise, a tendril at a time, all apparently on their way to full erection. Walt had a vision of an electrically shocked *Catweazle* crossbred with *Worzel Gummidge*.

But he was desperate and tried again. He had to be less circumspect. More demanding. Less polite. 'I am really thirsty. I need something to drink. Even water. . .this *is* an inn after all and you must-'

The old man gasped and scurried backwards, suddenly dropping out of sight behind the semi-circular bar. Only to pop up half of his head. Briefly.

'We're shut!' The head disappeared.

Walt was starting to appreciate the evidence of the rotten reviews on his *TikBox* for this *Drumhumble Inn*; he now wished he had taken at face value. He should have remained in his comfort in Norfolk. Safe Norfolk. *Sane* Norfolk.

A mumble rose from behind the bar. Now intelligible, slowly enunciated as if the old man was attempting to be if not hospitable then excessively courteous while self- translating from some other language. Probably Gaelic again. . .

'Frugal's nae, no', *not* here. And he'll be right carnaptious eh, in a really stinking, rotten, *right bad* mood when he comes back, returns like. . Always the same efter, *after*. . .a visit to Her. You dinnae, don't, *do not* want to come up against Frugal in a bad mood. Which is most of the time if truth be telt, eh. . . *told*. Frugal hates everybody. Foreigners in particular. And English yins worst of all. . .and especially after he's been to see *Her*. Ye can be siccar, eh sure, of that wan, *one* thing. . .Sir.'

Walt had spotted a curious small contraption in the middle of the bar top. It looked like a metal question mark. Brass by the looks of it. He watched it drip. It was a small tap. Water! Probably for customers to add to their whiskies. . .

'Go away!' the disembodied voice shouted. Then added, 'I dinnae want tae be here. Ah cannae stand the sicht o' blood!. . .eh, sight.'

In three short steps Walt reached the gizmo, turned the neat little lever from horizontal to fully vertical, bent forward, and turned his head to receive the gently flowing liquid fully into his mouth. It hardly touched the sides.

Never had water tasted so good!

He came up for air and bent for a second helping that was even better. Now he appreciated that this water *was* different. A herbal tang, a lovely lingering after taste. He bent for more unaware of his wild and wide-eyed audience who had risen at the sound of his activated tap.

'Ye've done it noo! Ya Sassenach eedjit. Oh, ye havenae half DONE IT!'

3

GRANNY'S PLANS GANG FURTHER AGLEY.

Frugal looked in vain for the invisible Force that had shot Granny from out of her Big Chair and caused her to stumble and hit her midriff in the corner of the kitchen table.

Through a severe winding she gasped and spluttered:

'Damn blast and bugger it all to Hades and back via the short cut! She paused, caught some breath. 'Twice! He's drunk it twice!' She collapsed against the table her hands scattering a couple of bowls, one of which spilled something that sizzled away adding to the myriad table scars.

Frugal was aghast.

He had never heard Granny swear but more worrying was the colour she had suddenly gone - from her usual light jade to a deathly grey.

'Whit is it, Granny? Whit's wrang.' Frugal moved to help the old woman, putting his arm around her narrow bony shoulders to gently walk her back to sit in the one big wing-backed tatty chair. Granny's Big Chair.

'Who are you talking about, Granny? Who drank what? "Twice", you said?'

This silence was a different silence. In the previous one Granny had been in control. A planned hiatus. Planned by her. Now she had lost it. Frugal had mixed emotions. The bastard in him which was usually his *force majeure* itched to exploit this opportunity to get what he wanted. But you didn't throw near enough fifty years of upbringing, if not a kind of surrogate maternal love, out the window just like that. Or did you. . .?

Frugal's rare wrestling with what passed for his conscience was terminated by Granny's words:

One-Sided Negotiations

'Oh, I knew days like these would come. She spoke as if Frugal were not there as she regarded the ceiling. 'First the Signpost, then the Portal, now the Water. The best laid plans are gone well past agley. . .and the grief and the pain are just beginning. . .'

Frugal was past aghast. Granny was crying. *Crying!* Swearing and crying. In the same day. At the same time!. . .

He briefly wondered if his demand for a break, a holiday had been responsible for this crack up. He almost felt guilty. Nearly. . . then the bastard in him won. Never give a sucker an even break. Especially a once all-powerful witch who had him tied to her yoke of running Drumhumble for all his adult life, but an old witch who looked like she was right now well past her worst. He didn't know whether to cry or laugh. He might just escape after all.

'So-' But that was as far as he got as Granny pushed herself upright, a determined look on her face. She walked slowly towards 'her boy' who now crumbled to perch on the footstool. She towered over him. Frugal cowered further, immediately dreading what was to come, knowing he was correct in fearing the worst. She had again read his evil mind.

'I planned to let you stew in your own juicy hubris a bit longer. But now there is an *emergency*. . .so. . . I'll make this quick, as it is *you* whae has the emergency to attend to.'

'In short:

One: you get your holiday. One week,' she said then mumbled to herself accompanied by her recovering normal cackle, '*that should be plenty. . .*

Two: But not until after 'All Eedjit's Day'. That's 6 weeks from now in case you were not counting.

Three: By then you'll have him up to snuff.' Granny raised a white and green eyebrow anticipating his question.

'Who? What-?'

'I knew you'd ask me that. You've already asked me-'

'What?'

'No, *Who?*

'What?'

'No, *Who?*! Asked me, *who?*'

For f-s sake...Frugal stifled his temper and the nascent imprecation and mumbled with a contemptible *sleekit(2)* attempt at simulated meekness that Uriah Heep would have coveted, 'I thought you were going to make this quick, dear Grandmother. He failed and blurted, 'O bloody K. . . WHO?!'

'Your replacement!' And dinnae be sae snippy.'

'What?!'

'No, *who*. The young fella's who's just drunk your water. Neat?!'

'Whit? I mean, Who? Where?'

'I was expecting a *Why?* Or at least a *How?* But one question at a time,' Granny cackled, chortled and eventually chackled. Her first chackle in ages, she realised. The physical apotheosis of her enjoyment: a hybrid cackle and chortle. The *chackle*.

She loved playing verbal ping-pong: because she always won. . .but she remembered the urgency. . . eventually.

'The Inn. Get back there. Now. I take you left Adonald in charge. I also take it that he forgot to lock the front door and him a Big Fearty. Couldnae stop your new trainee from gulping the neat bar water! Eedjit. Now I'll have to reschedule my Plan. . .Granny stared at the ceiling again seemingly oblivious to her thunderstruck visitor.

'Talk about a bad day. . .You still here? You have work – mucho - to do. Six weeks worth. Now I need peace and quiet. Here you'll need this. Then skedaddle! Allez! Pronto!.' Granny produced as if by magic (it was too) an opaque olive coloured vial from her much-stained smock and handed it carefully to him then shouted as Frugal rose.

'Now, Bugger off!'

Frugal scurried to the door yanked it open and tripped over Toby on the doormat.

The cat purred in satisfaction at the curses spat back at him from the now bleeding figure entangled in the lush and jaggy brambles.

The one thing Toby and Cocky agreed on was that they both disliked Frugal McDougal and not just because he was a rival for Granny's affections, but because he was a right nasty bastard. (Most of the time. Almost all the time.)

Granny's voice rang in Frugal's ears as he stood, staggered and bled.

'You better not have spilled any of my potion, Fergus McDougal! Otherwise, you'll pay for my new flagstones. . .out your wages.'

4.

WWW & FM

Frugal ran back to the Inn. He was angry and hurt but the prospect of even a week's escape acted as a spur and a wee bit of a salve.

As he reached the main street the few children running, late for school, gave him a wide berth as usual. Frugal hated everybody. Especially kids. Often thinking *King Herod wasn't all wrong* and almost as often shouting out this thought at them most times he saw them. And it was always his opening greeting when any youngster had the temerity to enter his Inn.

The kids felt his hatred and they reciprocated (to his perverted satisfaction) dreading any time their mothers sent them on an errand to the only shop in Drumhumble: the Drumhumble Inn.

He thumped open the Inn's front door so severely that it had no time for its normal protesting, creaking resistance.

Through the gloom he saw the figure slumped over his bar, next to the water spigot. His 'replacement'! This eedjit?! Passed out, overdosed, maybe dead, was Frugal's first and second thoughts. He wondered which condition he would prefer as he roared:

'ADONALD!'

The shuddering head rose from behind the bar, the long yellowish white hair billowing with the unaccustomed speed of ascent.

'Completely useless. . .were you just going to leave the puir wee man couped ower ma bar forever?'

'I didnae ken whit tae–' Adonald started to reply.

'Naw ye never do. Have to do everything myself. . . talk about keeping a dog and barking at the mess it makes of everything.'

'That's why ah waited for you, Mister McDougall. I kent ye wid want. . .ye ayeways say for me never tae touch anything.'

'Like the lock on the front phecking door?!' Frugal caught his breath, he would need to pay attention to his age. Nae mair running past 50. Christ, his heart was trying to burst out his second-best shirt. He leaned on the bar, calmed a little and glared at Adonald 'Oh pheque off ya eedjit, and gie me a haun. We'll stick him ben in number 2 until. . .*if*. . .he recovers.'

One-Sided Negotiations

Frugal checked his pocket for Granny's 'precious' vial then grabbed the body's hair and pulled it up to make the mouth fall open, shoved in the vial's vile contents then yanked the body half up to get his hands under its oxsters and nodded to Adonald.

'I'll tak the heid and you tak the feet.'

'And you'll be in the bedroom afore me? Adonald sang to the tune of 'Loch Lomond'.

Frugal grunted with the effort of lowering and carrying the body. 'A singing rotten comedian *and* completely useless. . .I don't ken why I-?'

But Frugal needed all his remaining breath for humphing this heavy wee nyaff(3) through to bedroom 2.

CHAPTER 5: LIFE AT THE INN.

1.

IT BEGINS

WALT CAME TO. In complete darkness. In some dank, musty-smelling place. On a bed, apparently. An uncomfortable bed.

He tried to sit up but cracked his head on what might be the ceiling, that he felt now only a few centimetres above him, his fingers tracing what could be rough cold cement. So, definitely it was not a bottom bunk bed and. . .no pillow, no bedclothes, no headboard; his fingers also told him of the narrowness and his feet almost overhanging told him of the short length. . .but he was fairly sure it was a small *bed* - it was certainly not King or Queen, definitely Commoner size. Not Royalty. Probably Serf, maybe Villein. He laughed despite his circumstances. Or perhaps because of them.

Walter Wilson Winston, aged 25, still slept with a comforting night light on in his one bedroomed Norfolk apartment: still scared of the dark. The dark had triggered that memory apparently. . . but somehow now the dark didn't frighten him.

And he did feel queer. Different. Detached. Strange. Like floating lying down, light-headed. . . like. . .like being slightly tipsy. He was never a good drinker - 'Can't- Hold It- Wally' had been just one of the many jibes in his adolescence, like other bullying barbs used by his post pubescent peers to rid them of his gloomy company, he just knew. He had figured it out since then. And recalled all of them. Often. Too often. By himself. On his own.

Strangely, right now he laughed out loud at the memories. Now. A real laugh. Now. And not the shiver or snort of embarrassment that those memories had always previously produced. Somehow, he felt like. . . if not a Winner, then certainly no longer a Loser. At worst a 'So-Whatter?'

Why? Maybe he was dead and in Heaven? And instead of being bathed in celestial light Heaven was a total blackout where you contemplated and scoffed at previously deeply wounding, scarring memories.

Heaven as *Perspective*?

He felt he should feel let down, conned, duped but he felt wonderful.

Why?

He remembered that all he had drunk was water. . .Water!. . . Out of the. . . Tap on the… Bar!

So, where was he now?

And why did he feel so. . .GOOD? And what was he wearing? It felt like wool. All wool from bare head to bare toe.

Strange his head did not hurt with that bang against the 'ceiling'.

He had to roll sideways trying to get up and out of wherever he was that he lay.

Was he in a cupboard? On the top shelf. . .he wished he could find a light. He realised that his fear of the dark really had left him.

He dropped to his knees and on all fours began groping the cold -- was it stone? - -floor hoping to find a wall. A wall with a door.

He finally found it despite the complete lack of light. He turned the handle and pulled. He was surprised that it opened, but more surprisingly he felt he would not have been worried if he had found it locked.

This feeling was. . whatever it was...a kind of *Carefree? Couldn't Care Less?* No that was *Indifference*. What was that French phrase *sans* something. . .*Suzie* or something. Whatever it was, Walter Wilson Winston wanted it to be a permanence from now on. . .

Forgetting Everything, Living in the Now, an Oceanic Feeling, Synhronicity, Connected to A Meaningful Universe. . .all those phrases Walt had frantically read in the umpteen Self-Help 'manuals', desperately seeking Peace of Mind, Escape from Guilt about moving out from his parents, not spending more time with them, before they died in that crash, constant business-building worries. . .Yes, all those terms that Walt had regarded as trite platitudes as far as he was concerned, states of mind that he felt he would never achieve appeared to have arrived. Together. All at Once. Now. The Wonderful Now. Forget Eureka. . .Hello Euphoria! He giggled then, thought,' Fuck the Lot of em!'

He heard an indistinct voice (maybe God's?) coming from -- what the glimpse of light at the far end suggested -- was a long narrow corridor. The faint light came from behind what might be. . . another door.

Walt, hands tracing the cold wall that was definitely stone, slowly made his way toward the tiny chink of light. It *was* a door. He stood there listening to the voice behind it.

> God's voice?
>
> Male.
>
> Loud now.
>
> Angry now.
>
> An angry God?

Waheh. . .?

2.

ALL IN A MORNING'S WORK

'Sit still, Niall. Christ's sake. You want to lose your other ear? Like the last time?' Frugal pulled his comb from his shirt pocket and attempted to stretch and flatten the cow's lick, preparing it for a healthy snip. 'Hells bells, it's a haircut! It *was* jist a short back and sides ye asked fur. Or dae ye want me tae have a check of yer auld teeth while I have ye in my Big Chair? That why you are hoaching? Sit flaming still wull ye!' Frugal further tightened the Big Chair's restraining harness as his customer attempted to wriggle free.

The customer grunted something loud and negative through a pain that Frugal was but vaguely aware of. His mind was way beyond immediacy of haircuts in this wee backroom in his Big Chair.

Frugal McDougal was deep into troubling thoughts about Granny and her 'deal'. A deal that involved the body in the bedroom that had been out for the count of nearly a day and a half since the last time he had sent Adonald to check. Frugal daren't check himself. He did not trust himself to be alone with the body, alive or newly dead, in the dark. . . who knows what urges might the Real Frugal Mcdougal succumb to?

Murder or. . .Worse?

Frugal was torn between trying to arouse, maybe resuscitate, the Incomer- Inncomer now - or letting him lie. Let sleeping problems lie – they might fade away. . .for ever. Aye, fade away. Snuff it. Like Frugal's dream of a holiday, a wee break, an escape maybe. But he quickly squashed that last thought hoping it had not had time to show up on Granny's radar. He vowed to never think the E word again. . .but he had just done it. Shite!

The Granny State of Drumhumble

The phone rang. The nearer one. Frugal stretched for it, ignoring the yell from the restrained recumbent protesting about the yank by the cow lick- embedded comb in Frugal's other hand.

'Did ye wait until I was busy, as usual, McCafferty?!' Frugal barked into the phone. 'Ye did ken it was Adonald's day aff I take it, aye. . . "Urgent"? Urgent ye say. "Urgent"?...Now what does that mean again? "Urgent"... Strange word. Unusual. Not one with which I am familiar. An alien concept ye might say to us Drummers, so why–' He listened briefly his face reddening from rapidly receding almost departed hairline to over-active lantern chin.

'Ye think I huvnae enough tae dae! Frugal exploded. 'Whit dae you fermer's think the Inn is? A phequing *garage*! Well, right, Mccafferty, imagine I am a typical fannying-aboot garage proprietor. . . I am pleased to inform you *we are still waiting for the part*. And so are you!'

Frugal slammed the phone down. Immediately the other phone rang. The further one, on the windowsill. He stormed over to it leaving his comb behind this time. The customer sighed in relief at the respite, however brief.

Frugal grabbed the phone. In a robotic tone he whispered, 'We are sorry we are unable to take your call at this moment in time as everyone has just gone into a meeting, this minute for staff training on customer care and attention that may take a few weeks or months, maybe even over a year, but your call is important to us.' Frugal hummed some *Musak* then paused before his bawl of valediction, 'But not important enough to ever call you bluidy back!'

He returned to his Big Chair, mumbling, 'Another fermer. Think they own the place. . . think I am at their beck and bluidy call. The smiddy is no' daft, no' tae get a phone in. Tam the blacksmith can get on wi' *his* work. *He* gets peace tae *specialise*. . .Me? Ah have tae dae *everything*.' He stopped and gazed in hatred at the Big Chair. He wished it was an

Life at the Inn

Electric Chair. And that he could throw the switch right phequing now. . .

But it was simply The Big Chair. His Big Chair in his wee backroom.

The backroom that was reserved for, haircuts, dentistry, minor surgery, first aid, secret meetings,(1) private functions, mini-ceilidhs, trials, inter alia, inter anything that paid. Cash - well Drumhumble Tokens. Drumhumble's own currency.

He reached for the comb that had remained in dangling situ in his restrained customer's hair, retrieved his scissors from his top pocket, determined to get by with this one task and concentrate on a strategy for dealing with Granny and the Backroom Body. But the phone rang. The nearest one again. But before he could reach it. The other phone rang.

Then a voice from the Bar (aka The Front Shop) shouted:

'Call yersel a Post Office?! There's nae bluidy bacon!'

CHAPTER 6: TRYSTING THE NIGHT AWAY…Part One

1.

Enter The Dominie (NOT Dominatrix. . .yet)

Toby the cat had mixed emotions.

There was the worry about GM 'losing it' – 'the plot'; 'the place'; the ability of precognition with her scrying and more prosaically, simply forgetting things: basic things like opening and shutting The Portal on time. (The last delivery of 'Vital Twenty-First Century Things' had ended up in the River Dread, along with their erstwhile reliable van driver who had quit for early retiral there and soaking then; *Spelled to Silence* regarding the village of Drumhumble of course. But just in time.)

Then there was Toby's felicitous feline frisson of a familiar's anticipation at the arrival of a visitor. Any visitor. But this was *not* just any visitor, this was hyper-frisson, uber-curiosity Toby was experiencing. The Great Granny Mulch had NOT anticipated this intrusion. GM was visibly flustered, disoriented, discombobulated. Toby did not like the sight, his feelings as ever in sync with his Mistress.

There was one thing about this, novel or not, Toby knew: to keep quiet. Well, there was one other thing. That clueless cockatoo: Cocky, would put her bird's Ozzie loud-mouthed ugly claw and beak in it sooner or later.

Toby shivered but then in delight stretched fully in the inevitable forthcoming schadenfreude and slunk under the Big Chair.

The cat did not have long to wait. She listened to Granny fumble and stumble over her words. Not a pretty sound.

'The dominie no less. . . or maybe that's *dominee*. . .*or domina*. . .*dominix* or phequing *domino* these days?. . . Well, well, my faithful Drumhumble schoolmistress and to what-' Granny was cut off.

This *was* unusual, Toby's eyes widened as he keeked out for a glimpse of this wonder.

'-It's time.' Eilidh McCrorie spoke softly. *Less was more*: her Drumhumble amateur dramatic experience had taught her *and* she had thoroughly rehearsed this performance. This was worse than any audition. It was crucial that she got what she had come for. And not just a part. She wanted the whole shebang.

Granny's Blessing. Granny's Help. It was time. Hopefully not past time. Granny frantically grasped at her scattering wits but she only experienced a murky picture, a slight notion and forming far too slowly. She looked Eilidh McCrorie in the eye.

Eilidh spoke again, each word slower, even softer. Her face sadder. No acting required now.

'It. Is. Past. Time. I was 37 six months ago. I am 37 and a half. Exactly. Exactly half way.'

Granny playing for whatever time it took to figure this visit out, grabbed at the first resort, from top of her witch's eclectic brew. *Flattery*.

'Eilidh. My precious Eilidh. I could not manage without you, for what is it now?'

'Twenty years.' A tear trickled from Eilidh right eye.

Even Toby the cynical cat could feel it. This *was* serious.

Toby was struck but Granny was still stuck. Flattery seemed not only to have failed but have made matters worse. Plan B. Second resort? No! Last resort.

Honesty.

'Eilidh, dearest, why don't you spell – sorry, spit -- sorry just *tell* me what...we are all girls together here-'

'Speak for yourself. Speak for yourself! Not the cat! Not the cat!' Cocky squawked.

Toby wanted to kill that bloody bird. Not by a long chalk for the first time but he settled for the half sight of Granny remarkably speedily struggling to her feet, grabbing the cockatoo's cage cover and swiftly blanketing and muffling the protests of:

'Gender bender! Gender ben-'.

2.

A KIND OF INDUCTION

'...And then there's the weekend. The usual: all night ceilidh on Friday until...later on; Saturday morning Kids Club - violent cartoons - exclusively Tom & Jerry; lunch time the Young Fermers weekly Chewing the Veg Meeting (Vegans only this week)...' Frugal after a quick gulp of air continued rattling off to a by now overwhelmed, cross-eyed and bemused Walt.

They were in the Main Bar. Frugal was still rattling on, all the while half- drying pewter tankards and hanging them on their hooks behind the bar. 'The early evening Saturday Big Film – this week a documentary on the Perils of International Travel - they tell me it is a right hoot, slapstick and other folk crashing burning and dying never fails, especially efter a two day delay at the airports – and then we wind down with the monthly late secret meeting of the Drumhumble Chapter of the Masons – a doddle - there's only two of them. And everybody kens who they are. And that daft wumman in the Eastern

Star is in the huff with me, so she'll no be bothering us wi her whines for "decent tea". '

Walt had stopped taking in any of this monotoned litany of Frugal's 'this week's work rota' - 'that might well soon be yours' - round about 'Tuesday Afternoon's Agenda': the ordering and receiving of a plethora of supplies; the drop- in dentistry in his Big Chair and the minor (and semi-major) injuries clinic combined with the Afternoon Teas – Grey (Earl) Tuesday Specials 'with a light saltire tint hair perm thrown in - all while you wait, petal'.

Walt's earlier euphoria was being steadily diluted by worry, incredulity and dread. It had been more than hinted that he was to be involved but he was still not certain as to *why* he, Walter Wilson Winston had been selected. Was it as pragmatic as being in the wrong place at the wrong time? This madman did not seem to like anyone but he detested Walt in particular. It was obvious even when Frugal was silent, the scowl and posture said it. Was this offloading of the pile of crazy duties a punishment? If so, for what? When he managed to get in a question, he would try and ask. Again.

'Whit's wrang, you are looking awfy pale. You need to lie doon again, Wally?' Frugal leered.

'My name is Walter, Mr McDougall. Walt if you-'

'Sorry my mistake. . .Walter is it?' Well mine is. . .Mister McDougal, Wally.' Frugal tried to simulate *Remorse*. It was as successful as his prior attempt at Concern. Just as phoney. Portraying either of these alien, ersatz emotions was bloody murder while an Id was screaming for its normal *lebensraum*, fair champing at the bit to be freed to roar at this faffing wee English bauchle to get tae Freuchie out of his hair, his inn, and his life.

Frugal had tried his best this whole Thursday afternoon: Simulation.? Dissembling? Common Courtesy? Politeness? Civility? Social (Phequing) Niceties? Frugal had a degree in none of these, had not even been close to attending one night class in any of them and he just knew this strain would sooner rather than later cause him to lose it and blow Big Time with a ferocious and vicious blast of The Truth. It was just a matter of time. . .

And if The Truth came out Granny would never release him.

But he already hated the sight of this wee shite.

Granny had charged Frugal with the price of his 'holiday': let Wally shadow and learn from him for six weeks until the day after Daft Eedjits Day; to have this effete Wally up to speed, enough to run the Inn for seven days and nights and-

Ach, was it worth it? Frugal asked himself yet again. A month and hauf of *this* for what? A week to recover! This unaccustomed ambivalence was a right bastard. . .

And Frugal knew *he* was a bastard (in every sense) and no way could a bastard like him be *nice*. Not for six weeks to a wee plooky plonker like this wally.

No, Fergus Ian Robert McDougall[1] would go aff his heid. His holiday would be one week and maybe the rest of his life in the Mental Ward in Raigmore: a Right Mess, in care of the NHS, in Inverness. If it still existed. If they still existed. The NHS *and* Inverness. . .the rumours of the plagues of the 2020s. . .

Time for a short cut, Frugal grinned, the evil abruptly unmasked and obviously scaring wee Wally further. Good! Two thirds of my life gone and six weeks of the last third wasted on this waster? No festering way!

Frugal felt better instantly, getting back to normal. You cannot fight Nature. (Especially when a sociopathic Nurture is deliberately laid on top.)

Time to call Granny Mulch's bluff.

He would either make a right erse of the Training of The Wally and be rid of the wee keech or maybe his ultra-harsh instruction would work a treat and a delighted Granny might reward him with more than a week's rest and recreation. . .

One way or the other it was a no-brainer. A win win situation for Frugal and a lose lose one for The Wally.

3.

DOMINIE v WITCH

The Life Force! Never to be trifled with. Not even by a witch. Not even by a witch firing on all spells, curses and potions.

Granny should have known, at least guessed. She *was* losing it: not only her powers of precognition but now Female Intuition. . .Hells Bells!

She looked Eilidh in the eye. Again.

Eilidh returned her look accompanied by a fey smile.

They both just knew. Now.

'Granny, I want a child.' Eilidh started over on her over-rehearsed monologue. 'I was grateful for your assistance last time. And I still am. Despite the outcome-. . .Or rather the lack of it. The-'

'Farce?' Granny couldn't help herself, shuddering yet again at her scryed picture that Eilidh need not have reported back of the *coitus non-commensus* of Eilidh McCrorie and her Fergus ten years ago. **(2)**

'Well they do say Pain plus Time equals Humour'. Eilidh gave a half snort then forced herself back to her 'script.' But Granny got in first:

'I am still so sorry about that. . .there are some things still beyond my powers to foresee. . .to arrange'. . .like firm, healthy lives after 75 years', then Granny added to herself *and the 'lackings' are becoming more every day*. But recognising or failing to recognise latent homosexuality was one of the least of her present worries. Foremost right now was trying to remember. . .something about this wee Walter. . .something that was now persistently pecking away at the back of her persistently migraine- nipping auld skull. . .

'No matter.' Eilidh half smiled. 'Water under the bridge as they say. Maybe 'twas meant to be. . . Granny, I know you have. . .well, specimens. . .in your jars -the frozen ones-'

'Eilidh my Eilidh. Never. You mean the emergency *semen*?' Granny was shocked.

'Yes. And this is an emergency. I am *just* the right side of forty years of. . .half my life is over!'

No!' I am never wasting your. . .*exposing,* your intelligent eggs, your protected ovaries, to the sperm of any one of the eedjits that donated it. By all that is unholy. . . the gene pool in this village is already on the brink of degenerate lunacy.'

'But. . .well, why keep the. . . stuff?'

'For *real* emergencies. Not-' Granny instantly beamed and blessed Necessity not for being the Mother of Invention but for providing the afflatus, this Inspiration.

No not inspiration, she *already* had had that! The memory was clear now. That was why she abandoned all her prejudices and detestation of that fernal (3) Internet and organised those spoof reviews on WWWWW's W. (4) This was how she had lured her Wee Walter here to her Drumhumble domain, And NOW she REMEMBERED… WHY HE WAS HERE!

'But. . .how am I?' Eilidh was on the verge of tears again.

'I have arranged for new blood to be brought into Drumhumble.

And New Sperm. . .'

Toby the cat bathed in the warmth of her mistress's restored smile due to her returned memory - however temporary, Toby initially cautioned himrself but decided like all normal cats (unlike burdened familiars) to try once again to 'live in the moment.'

4.

ATTEMPTED RECALCITRANCE

Walt's euphoria was long gone. He almost welcomed his worries that were trickling back along with his recent memory. It was probably the shock of this big bald buffoon's answer that had apparently restored Walt to sanity. The irony of the mounting insanity of Frugal restoring sanity in him at present escaped Walt.

'What kind of question is that, Wally? What de ye think I am? A philosopher? On top of everything else?'

'I only asked, "why was I here" and-?'

'You tell me.'

'But-'

'Why are any of us here, *chum*?'

'Well I remember. . .well getting lost in my car-'

'The revolving signpost, eh?' Frugal did not stifle a guffaw.

'Then I was right, I didn't imagine it?'

And then ye crashed yer motor car? Serves ye right. Evil, evil machines – that's one thing we dinnae miss. . .cos we've never. . .'

'Never, what?'

'That's for me to ken and you tae never know, Wally'

'Yes, I crashed and ended up in a river and-

'The River Dread. Bloody freezing they tell me.' Frugal's bad teeth(5) evidenced his mounting pleasure.

'Yes it was.' Walt shivered at the memory.

'But how did ye get. . .get *in?*' Frugal asked muttering to himself *as if I dinnae ken.*

'Well as far as I remember. I fell in. Backwards.'

'Why am I not surprised, Wally?' Frugal did not ask, snorted and lifted the cellar trapdoor.

'Cmon, Wally, doon here. Your crash course in Better Beer Management. Free gratis and for pheque all. . .'

'No!' Walt heard himself shout.

His memory felt fully returned. He was here on business. The business of checking those scathing reviews on his Website. And that Big Deal with the Big Hotel chain that was now no doubt in jeopardy. Goodness knows how long he had been in this madhouse?

'*No?*! No?! Whit dae ye mean naw?!' Frugal knew the Inn's tap water had finally worn off after the last three days. He might well have his work cut out. It would be a *pleasure.*

'I am a businessman not a cellar dweller.'

' Business Man is it? Business man ma chookies (6) Well this here is *ma* business. So,ye'll dae whit yer telt. Yer ma Trainee. THAT IS WHY YOU ARE HERE. . .Wally. You are doon these stairs! Noo!'

Frugal had had enough of this poultice's incessant questions. There was some of Granny's medicine left, enough to blank his memory and to put a stop to this festering pestering.

He had told Wally as much as he needed to know. Granny should be pleased that her 'Wee Fergus' had done as he was told. He might even get some days to add on to the week that couldn't come soon enough.

5.

A TEACHER'S WORK IS NEVER DONE

Eilidh McCrorie, teacher and reporter (7) and spinster was experiencing many emotions: some new; all of them exciting: each feeling caused by the successful outcome of her confronting Granny Mulch.

Roiling and rising now her feelings forced her to push her pile of marking for tomorrow's lessons to the far corner of her marking and dining table. The table was no longer used for entertaining. Not for ten years now. Not once. Not since The Frugal Fiasco. Her regulated routine was effectively controlled by Granny through her consistent, repetitive and predictable input and output of her charges and their evening marking workload.

Daytime she taught all the few Drumhumble kids in one classroom. All ages from 7 to 14: 8 years worth together. A yearly intake of 3 of 7 year olds and the 3 graduated out when they turned 15 to start work, and continue for the next 60 years. A few were apprenticed to vital, skilled work like 'engineering/blacksmith, milling, plumbing/electrical, carpentry/building, most went straight into unskilled tasks, mainly agricultural. Others stayed at home assisting their parents in the 'cottage industries', chiefly weaving. But all work, skilled or unskilled was 'arranged' by Granny guided by Eilidh as to their capabilities both mental and physical all to ensure the stability (aka *stasis*) of the Drumhumble economy and its way of life.

This year the one vital opening was for an apprentice blacksmith; someone to apprentice Tam at the smiddy, who, at 50 years of age had become a master smith on the recent death at 75 of the previous master; the previous apprentice at 30 was now made up to a journeyman smith. Young Fiona McClaverty would be the new apprentice.

Their first female blacksmith.

It had been touch and go to find a smart enough and strong enough apprentice blacksmith in time but Fiona would more than do. Girls not only matured quicker and quicker these days, they also matured *better*. Bigger. Stronger and often more intelligent.

Eilidh liked that and took not a little pleasure in Granny's mistake with the boy she had wrongly anointed at birth as a suitable smith.

The other 2, boys, this outtake, like most Drumhumble school leavers, were destined for general farm work: agricultural labourers to be fitted in wherever needs were greatest. Probably one would end up in the vineyards given this year's blight scare and the major restitution work now needed.

Eilidh knew, she should have faced up to Granny, laid her cards on Granny's huge kitchen table long ago. Not wait another ten years. Was nearly 38 too late to have a babby? She would only know by going ahead. And the sooner the better. The tock of her ticking biology would soon be deafening. Then silent. And Useless.

Granny had promised to arrange a 'meeting' with the intended father of her child as soon as she could. Eilidh had offered to speed up the 'process' – get 'It' over with as quickly as possible but Granny cautioned her. Men were 'difficult'. Unpredictable. Fickle. When it came to sex, some were even sensitive. Granny not so gently reminded her of the 'Last Time'.

Eilidh needed no reminder.

'The Fiasco' was burned deep in her memory. Up till now she felt scarred for life and doomed to be barren for her last thirty-seven and a half years.

For a long time after The Fiasco with that miserable useless object McDougal, Eilidh blamed herself. She felt she could have done more. *Granny* should have done more: to prepare her for her First. And Only...

Eilidh shrugged and shivered off the last rancid drips of the memory of ten years ago and then worried, wondering what measures Granny was going to take to guarantee 'The Union'...and the Conception.

The pile of marking on her kitchen table could wait. *Reading, Riting* and *'Rithmetic,* even Metal Work, Electrical Engineering, and Hand Loom Weaving were important but not as important as This.

She concentrated on imagining what Life would be like with a wee one to bring up. How much her Life and she would change...would *have to* change.

6.

IT'S USELESS TO TALK

Wally was back in the 'Back bedroom Number 2'. In bed at last. Exhausted physically but with his mind in overdrive and his body, *hoaching,* a word he would soon learn to use.

That hour in the cellar. Alone with Him. Had he imagined things? The creepy physical things: like being touched, the closeness, the hot stinking breath, the squeezing of his shoulders. All interspersed with barked orders, rattled instructions, hurled insults, delivered through anger bordering on. . . *Malice*? Or, was it simply the innkeeper's self-loathing? Hating what he really was and what was causing his ambivalent behaviour? A barely uncontrollable force that he had almost unleashed on Walt?

And no doubt there would be no let up tomorrow. McDougal had left him with a summary of tomorrow's work load that Walt was expected to share: Morning free coffees for Drumhumle's 74 year old women. His 'landlord' had stressed the age for some reason and he was somehow to check it; no doubt it was another Frugal bullying ploy – embarrassing him by demanding of old women their true ages. Then a long midday training stint in the out-shedded micro- brewery, after pushing a huge hand cart to and from the mill for the grain, to learn how to start a new batch of beer. Walt hoped his working environment in the out shed would be a lot less claustrophobic and threatening than that shuddering cellar experience. The afternoon was set aside for the quarterly meeting and trials of The Drumhumble Council -Criminal Division - with McDougal presiding as judge.

Walt was the nominated ingenue Jury. Late evening was for something else, something Walt had forgotten in his panic.

Things could only get worse.

Walt needed rescuing. He must get to one of those phones.

He managed it. The next mid-morning Frugal was at the dunny (outside lavatory), next to the small brewery. Frugal always took ages in there. Walt dashed indoors and surveyed the Main Bar, relieved to find the cellar trapdoor open. The idiot helper/hinderer, Adonald was down the cellar he could hear him wail:

'Have you ever heard the whip-poor-will? Da dum de dum too blue to fly.

Sweet dreams of you hoo...'

Walt grabbed the nearest of the two obviously ancient telephones, lifted the receiver, paused. How was he supposed to work this contraption? He only knew it was some kind of telephone because he had seen Frugal yelling into it.

But who would he call? Who *could* he call? A blast of desolation hit him like a physical force. Nobody. Nobody who cared. . . Except maybe The Authorities. . .kidnapping and slavery was illegal. . .wasn't it. Even up *Here*. . .

He eventually realised he had to spin the dial the machine. Three slow numbers. All the same - 9. To Walt this was a real emergency.

A woman's voice – old, by the barely discernible sound through the crackles - answered immediately.

'Adonald! Pit the phone doon this minute! If ah've telt ye once. . .999 has no place in oor Drumhumble Telephone Exchange! If it is an emergency -which I very much doubt, by the way - then use the ither phone. And for the Godforsaken umpteenth time, the emergency number is 666! And has been fir the interminable time I have been stuck up this bloody tree!'

Walt stared at the suddenly dead phone in his hand.

He dropped it on its base and leaped for the second phone on the windowsill.

7.

FRUGAL'S PHONISTRY (for thinking as well)

A strong breeze – the superstitious or those of a credulous disposition might deem it antiseptic – whistled through the knotholes in the tiny ancient wooden structure. Frugal was in the shiter at the bottom of the inn's long narrow garden. He was deep in thought. He managed his most profound thoughts, in squats, sometimes with the trots. His shiver had nothing to do with the cool breeze dissipating and surrounding him: it had no physical source, it was purely mental aggravation.

Today was no exception, in fact his thinking had reached as serious a depth as he could go, had ever been. Was this *his* male menopause? Ten years later than Outside? If so, it was typical of Drumhumble where most things were 'extended': summers, harvests, now menopauses. Most things but not Lives. Unless you termed 75 years an extension. . .three scores years and ten plus an extra five. Not for good (or bad) behaviour but for the guarantee. The guarantee of never suffering major sickness or illness in those 75 years and escaping the myriad horrors of old age. No cancer, multiple sclerosis, no motor neurone disease and no *carers*, no mental decrepitude, all of them apparently more and more on the increase Outside. Forecasts of nearly 3 million dementia sufferers by the time Frugal hit 75. And 75 hit him. He had watched the documentary films as he had projected them to the whole village at one of the monthly Saturday night showings.

Frugal's ponderings had ranged through The Past with his birth and Granny's upbringing to the Present with his ridiculous workload and lack of time to himself. But mostly he thought about The Future. From birth everything had been controlled by Granny Mulch. Like everything else in Drumhumble but only *her* Fergus had received the full treatment from birth. Up close and excruciatingly personal. Could he escape that fate continuing in the 25 years he had left if he remained in Drumhumble? No! But would he be any better off outside Granny's cocoon? Outside?. . . If he ever got that 'Holiday', would he come back? Would he want to? But his destiny maybe lay Outside. His real mother maybe was still There? And even his Father. . .

He shook his sore head trying to clear and free it – too many hard thoughts - and another uncontrollable fearful tremor accompanied it, but he resolved to take a last roll of the dice, push to the limit what he now decided was an opportunity with 'his shadow', Wee Wally and reached for the top neatly quartered sheet of the monthly 'Drumhumble Drum' nailed to the back of the privy door. He took care to present his erse with the Deaths section, in particular the notice of the demise of that pompous prick of a blacksmith.

'Aye it's an ill wind and all that,' he said thinking it was time he visited the new blacksmith, Tam – the closest to a friend Frugal had.

8.

IN THE NAME OF THE WEE MAN

The second phone to Walt looked identical. Despite his turmoil, he remembered the telephonist woman's instructions to whom she thought was old Adonald – 'use the other phone and dial 666'...

He did.

'This better be guid, Adonald! If you are messing me aboot again-'

'This is not-' Walt knew he had to be quick but he was not rapid enough to finish his plea.

'In the name o' the wee man, *who is this*?! Ye sound furrin. Bloody English too, if I am not mistaken and I am nut. Never! No' wi accents. Jenny McSmith-McJones is renowned for her ear for accents. I might be getting oan, but I can still tell wan end o' the village fae the ither; can still determine a ferm labourer's verbal nuances fae the speech patterns o' the carpenter and the builder, can still discriminate a handloom weaver's colloquy fae a miller's; a blacksmith's chat fae a seamstress; a dyers-'

'My name is Walter Winston!'

Walt screamed in desperation, one eye on the back door, the other on the trap door. (No mean feat without a strabismus.)

There was a silence. Perhaps blessed. But before Walt could continue-

'And whit the hell is Walter Winston, Englishman – polite, mind you, I'll give you that – doing on Frugal McDougal's emergency phone, pray?'

The woman's accent had dramatically altered to match Walt's, Norfolk shades, included. Maybe it was her job to make callers, users, feel comfortable? But the next verbal blast dispelled such fanciful thinking, being delivered with exaggerated Received Pronunciation although still with tints of Norfolk.

'One takes it that the aforesaid Frugal McDougal is unaware that his, shall we say, 'guest' is having the temerity to partake in the use of the aforesaid instrument or should I simply ask for thou to putteth the aforesaid Mister McDougal on the fornicating line?' She appeared to pause for breath.

Walt jumped in.

'I am. . .I want you to connect me to the *police*. I have been captured. I am being held here-'

Trysting the Night Away... Part One

'- *against your will*? Would it be? I take it you are, may I say, youthful. It does take a long life to be anathematic to and with clichés, after all. But I estimate that not only are't . . .thou, or should I say *is't* thee young, thou are't or is't, *naïve*. And if I could see you, I would say that you not only sounded stupid but you would *look* exceedingly intellectually challenged. Oh it's good to talk-'

'Look, will you connect me to the police or-'

'Regional, national or Interpol?' she boomed, back in her local accent.

'Any!'

'Sorry, this is the Drumhumble Exchange. Local calls only. AND ONLY FOR LOCALS!'

Walt stared at the second phone. Dead now like the first

CHAPTER 7: GENESIS (of sorts…Auto?)

1.

REGRETS? A Few…

GRANNY MULCH'S MIND was wandering off on its meandering ways through her unique synapses.

Her concentration was definitely worse. Was this typical of senility? Being unable to focus on current important duties due to the invasion of seductive thoughts of yesteryear. And she had many a yesteryear to mull over -- regrets that never left and made her wonder how her life could have been different.

Like 1645: if she had not run away: from Matthew Hopkins the self-styled Witchfinder General and his scourge of East Anglia; his condemning of over 300 alleged witches in the space of two short years. She could have remained and hidden out in her native Norfolk but no, she had fled, terrified of being put to the duck pond and its inevitably terminal 'swimming test'.

The irony hit her again: by the time she had found and settled in Drumhumble, Hopkins and his henchman Searle or Stearle (she could not remember now) had retired and witch hunting had been virtually 'outlawed'. Gone from Norfolk anyway. Like her.

In the many years travelling, always for some reason north, she had finally discovered the village of Drumhumble. A village not much smaller than it presently was – not much changed she now realised as she thought back these 385 years. The Inn was as central to life then as it was now. And the Inn was where she had found shelter and a post as a 'serving wench' - eventually Innkeeper and finally owner. (with the really short life expectancy in those days Granny Mulch had

Genesis (of sorts...Auto?)

little trouble in outliving the highly mortal locals and thus establishing herself in her central position of Wise Woman with The Power.)

But she was being silly. Would her life have been any better had she stayed and hid in Norfolk? Would she have developed the Powers she did? She doubted it. And would she have been as important, so vital to the, if not the flourishing, then certainly the preservation (and protection) of this village now so dear to her heart -- for the best part of four hundred years. She could never have loved Norfolk as much as Drumhumble. . .

Instead of wondering what might have been she should think of all her achievements – all her *saves*. Or more accurately her '*Savings*' Like saving the whole village from those despicable genocidal Highland Clearances; like saving all the young men from constantly being hauled off to War – wars in The Americas, Europe, South Africa, Korea, Africa, Malaysia, the South Atlantic, the Middle East. . .*inter alia*.

The Scottish Soldier was always the first call.

But there would never be a need for a war memorial in her Drumhumble. . .over her dead body. . .

She blanked that last thought and thought instead of all her other achievements in Drumhumble. They mounted, coming up to date with saving her 'Drummers' from all the Modern Perils of Outside, the chief of which were motorised vehicles, computers and pandemic plagues.

Chernobyl's fallout or more precisely her anticipation of it in 1986 had indeed been a blessing in disguise as far as she and her Drummers were concerned. The effort and time she had put in to mentally finally fully erect The Shield, from its wall-like beginnings to ward off the first horseless carriages (*damn and blast Henry Automating Assembly Line Ford*) had been more than worth it. Drumhumble's street had never seen a motor car; nor its air the carbon monoxide pollution. The World Wide Web, Mobile Phones and Social Media were as unknown to her Drummers as that Acid Rain since completion of her Scutum. . .

Granny chuckled, cheered up now, no longer regretting banning tractors, relishing the purity of horse drawn husbandry and realising she was in danger of being a silly old woman. . .c'mon, Nikkie girl, get a grip. . . think of *her Drumhumble*, forget Norfolk.

'Norfolk!'

She shouted waking both cat and bird who had both uncharacteristically been asleep at the same time. Norfolk was important for some reason. Not a four hundred year old reason but a current one. . .

'C'mon!' she urged her memory…

'Where to? Where to?' Cocky demanded.

But Toby knew not only when to be quiet but also when to speak. A familiar knew just enough to know Granny's agitation had to do with *The Inn-Comer*'.

'Wally.' She purred softly, but not quietly enough. . .

'Arsehole! Arsehole!' delivered as it should be in an authentic north Australian accent.

'Wally!' Granny almost leaped out of her seat, a smile quickly forming.

'Am not! Am not!'

'Are so! Are so!' Granny said reaching for the cage's shroud. 'But you are not, good Toby. . .'

Granny's mind rapidly connected, Norfolk with Wally (one of the reasons she had picked him – an innate sense of synchronicity

Genesis (of sorts…Auto?)

perhaps?) and just as quickly moved to item One on her To Do List (Urgent):

Item One: The 'Introduction' of Master Walter Wilson Winston to Miss Eilidh Isla McCrorie.

CHAPTER 8: COURT

1.

JUDGE AND JUROR (and Usher/ Macer)

OVER A WEEK enslaved and no nearer escape. Walt had temporarily given up on getting back through IT; four furtive fruitless forays by moonlight to all four points of the compass had ended the same. A brick wall, or as good as, coming up against IT. What with these long treks and the daily forced labours Walt had never known such tiredness: chronic fatigue more like.

But this afternoon it would be a mental task not physical he faced.

Jury service.

He was 'appointed' to be the sole juror in a series of trials of some accused villagers. He was the jury appointed by Frugal McDougal the self-appointed (well, by Granny) judge. And the first trial was due to start in a few minutes.

Walt had asked about the alleged crimes but was told in certain terms:

'Ye'll fin oot soon enough, Frugal had said. Jist mind tae dae as yer telt. . .an we'll get oan jist fine, Wally boy. And if ye play yer part right. . . might even be a wee reward in it…like a lie in, in the morn.'

Walt watched Adonald put the finishing touches to the inn's surprisingly spacious backroom. The low brown beamed ceiling disguised the deceptive space that itself was enhanced by the now almost complete lack of furniture or fittings. The windowless room lit by a few judiciously sited flickering electric sconces added to the ominous aura.

Adonald as ever, when alone, was singing to himself, unaware of Walt having just entered from his back bedroom. The old man was busy, bent over a broad central table, his back to Walt.

'Ten years ago on a cold dum dum

Someone was shot by the dum de dum

The judge said son you-'

Walt, desperate to find out something, *anything* about what was too soon to be in front of him, made the mistake of interrupting Adonald. And scaring him. . .and not for the first time these last days.

'Adonald, about this-'

'Aaaagh! Whit the pheque. . .?!'

'I'm so sorry. . . didn't mean to scare you. It's-'

'-Should be a law against creeping-'

'-I wasn't-'

'-It's you that should be on the Wee Stool there. No' the likes o' daft wee Sandy McGreggor. . . you, creepin aboot gieing folks flegs!'

This was a breakthrough for Walt – near actual communication with Adonald. All the many previous attempts over this last long knackering week, like those about getting out of here, escaping, had met another brick wall. Walt decided to nurture this apparent development. He had noticed a recent thaw in their relations; the old man's grunts and mumbles in monosyllables had softened from scared to wary, but never directly answering one of Walt's many questions, when the two of them were together and well out of Boss Frugal's earshot.

It was time for Walt to exploit this change, a change probably due to the old man becoming reluctantly used to, maybe inured to Walt's presence. Yes, he would if he could, get Adonald to answer at least *one* question and take it from there. One answer at a time. . .

'Flegs?' Walt asked softly.

'Aye. Gieing folk flegs. . or as you might pit it "frightening the shite", no, "*shit* oot o' them". From day one. . . nae wonder Frugal and you are sae close.'

With that the old man turned his back again and reached for a bundle of nearby papers and began to arrange them into small, neat, separate piles on the large central table that separated the huge, throne-like chair from a tiny stool. The only two pieces of furniture – named, as it turned out, The (Frugal's) Big Chair (of Justice) and the Wee Stool (of Shame). (When not used for milking.)

Walt wondered if the old man was jealous, resenting an imagined relationship between Walt and his boss – a relationship that *was* close. Close to slavery. (and too close to buggery?). With no choice, if Walt wanted bed and fed. Or maybe again, God forbid, Walt was being trained to be Adonald's successor. . .but he was determined to find out what this afternoon held for him.

'Sandy McGreggor was it. . .you mentioned. Adonald, is he-'

'Nane o' yer business!' The old man spat on the stone floor and rolled and ground the ball of viscous phlegm into the dust all the while mumbling about 'bloody nosey parkers creeping aboot. . .bleddy furriners as well tae boot. . .aye boot. . .boot them oot. . .and birch them aforehand. . .Aye. '

'But it is my business!'

The old man slowly turned and glared balefully.

Walt's resolve began to crumble.

'Mister McDougal. . .Frugal. . . has appointed me. . .eh. . .I am the jury!' Walt eventually blurted.

Adonald wheezed and spluttered, his incredulity and glee increasing in concord, holding his sides now as he burst into raucous cracking whoops, his body bending forward then straightening, wracked and shaking with every new burst of uncontrollable laughter. He slowly calmed a little then spoke through lingering spasms of apparent joy to an increasingly perplexed and worried Walt.

'Jury. . .jury. . .jury be Christ. Ye might have warned a'body.'

'Why?'

'Ah could've selt the tickets. . .'

At that Frugal McDougall came in from a side door. He was wearing a bright blue poncho-like cape with gold trimmings, one hand and arm, holding a pint of his own brew extruded incongruously revealing the ubiquitous Drumhumble checked woollen shirt - the uniform apparently of the few adult male Drumhumblers Walt had come across this long week.

The incongruity of Frugal's garb was completed if not complemented by a perky precariously perched plum beret three sizes too small for his large, largely bald head.

2.

BARELY PRELIMINARIES

'Right! Chop chop.' Frugal plumped down into the Big Chair, deposited his pint safely on the right hand arm rest then revealed his other tartan checked arm to run his left hand lovingly along the splendidly thick oak chair arm leaving both arms there – a king at home on his throne. Or *emperor*, given the toga-like apparel.

'Move it, old man. Today. You. Adonald, usher and macer. Mind? Me judge and - ' Frugal paused, as if suddenly aware of Walt and puzzled by his presence.

The Granny State of Drumhumble

'Him. Jury' Adonald wheezed and chackled **(1)** his slow exit to the front public bar.

Walt began to leave, heading for the asylum of his bedroom hoping he had misunderstood Frugal yesterday and that he was not needed.

'Where dae ye think. . .the lavvy's that way. Frugal pointed towards the tap room door. Nervous are't thou, wee Walter. Perfectly understandable. Big responsibility deciding some poor wretch's future. . .and fate.'

Walt stammered, 'Where do you. . . should I. . . stand?'

'Dae ye see any mair seats? Unless you want the Wee Stool of Shame. Some sin ah dinnae ken aboot? Get it aff yer chist. . .?

'No, I mean. . .eh. . .where do you *want* me to stand?'

'Anywhere ye like. As long as it's oot o' harm's way -- your harm that is. Some of these Drumhumblers do take offence at some of ma harsher sentences. . .showing their displeasure by resorting to actual physical violence. . .and today's cases look particularly menacing.'

As if on cue a hub bub arose from the direction of the tap room, the sounds of many voices arguing, mostly rough and male, interspersed with a singular throaty female shriek, and all competing with the rising protests of Adonald.

Frugal raised his left hand to cock his ear, a malevolent smile began to form. Malice – definitely aforethought -- coupled with satisfaction.

'And we've no even started. . . I kent it was a braw decision to involve you, young Walter. Consider it but part of your. . .your induction, a crash course, ha ha. . .Walter you are my back up. I can tell you that last court session was. . .let's say a close-run thing. . .too close for comfort. My comfort. . . I mean the temerity. . .contesting Judge McDougal's right to. . .after all I've done for the ungrateful pheque-wits. . .wan o' them had the nerve tae accuse me of being a bluidy dictator. . . *Dictatorship*?!. . .well no' the day they willnae. Today, dictatorship nae mair, Drumhumble, welcome tae *Democracy*. And that's where you-'

Frugal was interrupted by Adonald scurrying in, hair wisps awry with the unaccustomed speed of movement as he shouted back over his bent shoulder towards the racket that was a hub hub no longer: it had risen rapidly through brouhaha and fracas to closer to rebellion and revolution, right now a full blown (what he would learn to term) Rammy.

'Nae use getting carnaptious wi me! A dinnae mak the rules!' Adonald shouted.

'Naw! Ye jist back them up!' That same strident female shriek.

'See that Bella McGreggor. . .' Adonald shook his head half in despair as he faced his master, Frugal, but Walt caught a secret, satisfied smirk of Adonald's as he turned to look at Walt.

Frugal raised a bushy eyebrow. 'I take it Bella didnae take too kindly tae her wee hauf wit Sandy being placed last in the queue.'

'Ye could say that-'

'I jist did ya eedjit. It wisnae a real question it wis a-'

'Restoreakil-'

'Near enough-'

'Ye've learned me often enough,' the old man looked proud as he reached for the nearest papers on the Big Table and handed them to his boss.

'No nearly enough, apparently. . .Enough! Wheel in the first victim!'

Adonald puffed his way out again as the Judge boomed:

'Let's be having the knicker-knocker!'

4.

A (the) Juror speaks

It had been, if not an education, at least an eye-opener for Walt; it was certainly a quick insight into the darker side of this weird village - from the penchant for purloining petticoats from a next door neighbour's washing line through a case of public disorder where the drunkenness exposed the more serious crime of home brewing beer and poteen distilling threatening the Dumhumble Inn's established monopoly of alcohol, to that last case of sibling incest – 'family phequing' as the charge sheet had it.

All three cases resulted in Judge Frugal handing out hard labour sentences in the lush fields surrounding the village. Apparently, it was no coincidence that this court had been held in the run up to the many imminent harvests; the tobacco crop seemingly required significant supplements for its labour- intensive harvesting.

Through all this, Walt had been ordered by Frugal to say nothing, to simply watch and learn, but now just before this last case he was receiving instructions.

'Listen and listen good, Walter. Your time has come. Big moment this. Hello democracy. And pheque you, Bella McGreggor.' 'Bella' as in bellicose, Walt wondered. . .

Frugal grinned an aside to Adonald who started to smile and chackle. 'Aye pheque you, Bella McGreggor', Frugal repeated, 'and the Clydesdale you rode in on. . .wi yer wee eedjit grandson oan its the back.' He turned from addressing Adonald to Walt.

'Whatever I do and say, your simple task is to nod, agree and say "aye" or "agreed"'.

Walt nodded nervously.

'Steer em in Macer!' Frugal barked at Adonald who scuttled to a far corner to produce from behind the dusty olive-green curtains what looked like a large ceremonial wooden club then scurried happily to the door to the taproom but stopped and turned with a perplexed look.

'Is this no' an *Usher's* joab? Ye said 'Macer', eh Fr, eh, Mr, eh, Judge?'

'At least ye remembered *ma* joab. You are *baith* Macer and Usher, mind? You really need yer short-term memory sorted. I'll make an appointment wi Granny Mulch early next week-'

At that the old man screamed and started shaking 'Naw, dinnae, ah'm sorry. Ah'll nae forget again, Judge.'

'See ye don't. Now round up the clan McGreggor. . .or whit's left of it.'

Walt made a note to find out more about this Granny Much. He would wait to get Adonald on his own. . .Walt knew better than to ask Judge Frugal who right now was rubbing his hands and stretching his shoulders and neck in anticipation of meeting 'the McGreggors'.

Walt worried more about his neck and his particular role in this farce.

5.

Meet the McGreggors (what's left of them)(and the Court Reporter)

Walt could tell even before it started that this last case was different from the previous handful.

This time there was more than the accused in 'court'. There were two more: both women. One stood beside the Wee Stool looming over her tiny grandson with a protective fleshy, heavily muscled and mottled bare arm on the boy's shoulder accompanied by a fierce scowl, now more a death stare, directed at the Judge.

The other younger woman had come in, unushered, to stand well back from the proceedings and against the opposite wall from Walt. She looked directly at Walt and smiled. Walt felt himself begin to redden but briefly smiled back.

The older woman, Granny McGregor, obviously scared Adonald as he had kept her at more than arms-length the whole way to the Wee Stool. Walt too felt frightened, increasingly so. This was an enormous woman.

He wondered if the sarcastic look on Judge Frugal's face masked not a little trepidation in the face of such obvious animosity, despite the protection of the Big Table and the elevation of his Big Chair.

The contrast of the other woman with the grandmother could not have been greater. This woman exuded neatness, slimness, gentleness and a mature beauty despite her flustering as she produced a large notebook and apologised to 'the Bench'.

'My apologies-'

'Yer here. That's bad enough. Dinnae prolong this any mair than is needed.' Frugal obviously did not like this woman either. His quick glare seemed more hateful even than that he now held on Granny McGreggor.

The woman did not seem fazed by the judge and as she stood with a pencil poised ready at her pad, she looked directly at Walt and now gave him a wink and a bigger, gorgeous smile.

Walt's blush this time did not go unnoticed by the Judge. This rushed more blood to Walt's face.

'And when ye've quite feenished flirting, nay tampering with the jury – if this wisnae such an important occasion that deserved recording and publicised in 'The Drum' I would be of a mind tae chuck ye oot. . .Clerk of Court! Read the charge!

Walt could appreciate Adonald's confusion as the old man frantically looked around under Frugal's mounting fury. None of the previous cases had had a charge read, nor had witnesses appeared, all accused had meekly subjected themselves to the summary justice and subsequent sentences of hard agricultural labour.

'Clerk!' the Judge boomed and glared at Adonald who now started to shake, and stammer:

'Ah but. . .ah but. . .

'Ye think this is a monastery?! I am a judge and 'you are the clerk of-'

'-But ye said ah wis the usher. . .and the macer, mind? Ah've never-'

'Wheesht! Dae it masel. Like everything else!' Frugal turned from Adonald, to the Reporter, maintaining his angry face and barked 'Ye can start now, dear, and strike anything ye've pit doon already or contempt of court or for court will be the least of yer worries!' He turned back to Adonald, indicated the last papers isolated on the Big Table, and enunciated loudly, 'Ush -er. . .the charge papers p-ul-lease.'

Adonald happily obliged, scurrying, as the Judge adjusted his tiny plum beret that had been in danger of slithering down over his wrathful face. He took the shaking papers and slowly smoothed them out when Granny McGreggor snarled:

'Aboot bluidy time an all.'

'Silence in court!' barked the Judge as he produced a large wooden mallet from under his bright blue cloak and thumped the arm of his Big Chair.

Walt snuck a look at the attractive woman but she spotted him and gave him that smile – even warmer and lovelier. This time Walt was in luck with his 'beamer' as the Judge was too intent on reading the charge.

'Sandy McGreggor, you are charged with public indecency and bestiality how do you plead?'

'How can he plead ya stumer?! (2) Granny McGreggor's laugh was betrayed by her fiercer look.

'Language! This court will have respect!' the Judge hammered.

'Language. . .respect. . .yer erse!' Granny spat on the floor.

The judge hammered to no avail as Granny shouted over him; eventually it was as if the noise was an accompaniment, almost a tympanic emphasis.

'The boy is only nine and ye come oot wi words like *bestiality* and *public indec*ency, how is he meant to. . .ach yer head's fu o' mince, ya baw bag (3) . . .ayewiz hus been. . . you of aw people in this village should ken whit it's like tae no huv ony parents. . .but aw naw. . .'

This last argument, a kind of *ad hominem* seemed to register with the judge whose judicial hammer paused in mid thump.

'Enough.' Frugal's voice quietened. Curiously this silenced the irate grandmother. Perhaps she knew she had gone too far or maybe had got through to the judge who continued in softer tones. Relatively.

'Last time ye accused me of being a dictator. This time it seems ye have cast me in the role of. . .whit?. . .uncaring tyrant?. On the first charge I listened – hence the presence of an impartial jury. A neutral, an impartial. . . Outsider-'

'Him? That's yer jury? Dinnae make me laugh.'

Walt's worries returned and mounted geometrically perhaps algorithmically.

'As I was saying before I was so crudely interrupted – An impartial Outsider, who shall have the final say in any verdict or sentence. And on today's charge against me of being unfeeling. . .why don't we hear. . .*briefly*. . . what the accused has to say. . .and we'll take it from there?'

'Wee Sandy has asked me, me, his granny, and guardian ever since his parents were taken from us at too early an age in a tragic calamity-'

'Okay. Okay. We are aw greetin noo, minding how they baith got 'baled' mid harvest. Did ye never think it's God's retribution for instead of bringing in the sheaves they used them for indulging in mahochmagandy?'(4) the judge suddenly turned to the reporter 'Strike that last remark!or. . else!' Back balefully, to Granny McGreggor he said, 'Carry on, but as Rasputin or John Wayne might pit it. . .*gonnae cut to the chase*?!'

'My grandson's defence,' Granny adjusted her considerable bosom upwards with folded arms, 'is that every laddie does it and none of them are in here up before ye plonked on this Wee Stool of Shame. . .where's the shame? It's only natural at his age, the age of galloping hormones and ah am pretty damned sure ye indulged in it yersel. . .*Judge*, when ye were his age. . .probably still-'

'Neither here nor there. . .and certainly not twice a week. . .and never in broad daylight nor in the village square. . .and never with a *ram*! Christ's sake wumman, Mcfarlane's prize blue riband stud is ruined for life it. It disnae ken which end is whit-'

'Blethers! A wee potion fae Granny Mulch and McFarlane's ram'll be right as rain. . .and ye cannae expect a confused ignorant wee laddie tae recognise the admittedly considerable knackers on that brute. *But only when viewed from the side.* Anyway, the beast will soon enough remember whit's its danglers and the rest of him is fur when GM remodifies him.' With-'

'Guilty. But extenuating circumstances. Grandmother to fully explain the facts of life -- including decent and proper sheep-shagging to grandson -- that said, sentenced to one half day bringing in the sheaves and let's hope Wee Sandy has better luck in the field than his mammy and daddy.'

The judge looked at the grandmother who briefly nodded and patted her grandson on his head.

Frugal stood as if proceedings would be closed by one blow of his Big Hammer but held it aloft, suddenly remembering:

'May I ask for the Jury verdict. . .on the verdict?'

Walt eventually stammered 'Ag- agreed.'

'And the sentence?' The judge smiled horribly.

'Agreed.'

'Case closed.'

BANG!

CHAPTER 9: THE NIGHT AWAY…at last…mibbe.

1.

ONEPLAY

WALT CURSED THE second lot of hand me down clothes that Frugal had chucked at him. He considered asking Adonald but dismissed the idea of the old man's cast offs being any more suitable than Frugal's for his date.

His first date.

And the *woman* asked! Asked *him*. The super-attractive court reporter who had boldly introduced herself as Eilidh McCrorie and had asked him, he, the jury, to visit her and all under the disgusted eye of Judge Frugal.

He hoped the reason she had asked him was not simply to be 'an interesting subject' of an interview for her local newspaper. . . no, she had asked him 'to call on her' and at 'my wee cottage, next to the school.' Surely there was more to it than being 'strictly business'. . .?

Walt almost refused to worry about the fact that she seemed to know that Frugal would give him the evening off and 'a wee lie in' tomorrow. Surely, they were not in cahoots? Not that ogre, the beast. . .no Beauty and the Beast was only in fairy tales. Surely, she couldn't be trying to make Frugal jealous, but there had been an air of her rubbing Frugal's nose in it for something.

Whatever, Walt was excited and not a wee bit afraid.

The Granny State of Drumhumble

Turning up the heavy woollen trousers and making yet another new hole in the well-worn leather belt would have to do. He had almost lost his wee pot belly with the vegetarian food and the tough exercise. . . Great!

And the shirt though freshly cleaned was exactly like the one he had put aside for washing, both at least three sizes too big. Even if he had a tie, it would not go with the dull tartan pattern never mind the fact that the gap between his Adam's apple and the collar could allow the entry of an additional wearer. He wondered again what had happened to the smart striped business shirt he had arrived in not to mention the suit trousers, underwear, socks and shoe.

But things were looking up. It seemed that Judge Frugal was at least satisfied with his performance as The Jury and. . .now he had a date. A date!

Walt felt his luck had returned, probably a reward for all he had endured on the final miles of his journey plus the hard labouring with casks and barrels and dodging Frugal -- especially in the cellar. And that long lingering look of Frugal's when Walt had stood nakedly cringing before him still made him shiver, clothed now or not.

Walt wondered if he should 'borrow' a bottle of wine from the bar or cellar to accompany his visit, his date, and the lady's promise of 'a wee bit supper – nothing fancy, just finger food' but decided the likely discovery and certain wrath of the innkeeper was a risk too high.

Maybe he should pick some suitable flowers on the way through what he remembered of the remarkably fecund environs of Drumhumble?

2.

TWOPLAY

Eilidh, the very occasional reporter, and full-time teacher as she had explained just earlier took a note now and then as she sat opposite Walt. Walt could imagine their knees touching, the space between his chair and her two-seater sofa being so little. The whole cottage was small, both outside and inside, built for one, Walt briefly imagined Eilidh re-named as Wendy. The house was beautifully maintained outside and immaculately neat from what he could see of the interior.

Walt mused and dreamed while he told his saga, and most of all taking in the attractive woman: jet black hair in a bob, beautiful skin that did not appear to have a vestige of makeup, a neat tartan shawl that failed to disguise her pleasing curves, tanned slim legs emerging crossed from a mid-length multi coloured skirt, all in natural harmony but for the jarring pink fluffy slippers that she had earlier apologised for, due to her 'bad feet'.

' Can I ask-'

'No questions, Walter. Later. Then I'll answer all your. . .well all I am able to.' Her smile grew. She had anticipated him. Again.

Walt had read of 'spey wives' with 'second sight'. Was this gorgeous lady one of them? Walt was unsure whether or not this added to her attractiveness.

'Go on, Walter, please finish your. . .tale.'

'Well, that's about it. Apart from all the work, hard graft under Mr McDougal of the. . . last. . . week, I think it is. . .'

Eilidh smiled at him. 'Nine days to be exact. That would be the river Dread. The waters do that to Outsiders. Shock away the memories. Whoosh! Just like that. Gone-'

The Granny State of Drumhumble

'For ever?' Walt wasn't sure what answer he wanted. And how did she know it was exactly nine days he had been in Drumhumble? He had not ventured out from Frugal's yoke until only four days ago. And only in the dark. Trying to find a way back through IT. . .

'Ah, that depends. . .' Eilidh smiled, her dark brown eyes sparkling.

'On what?' Walt became uneasy; and not like the nervous anticipation when he had knocked on the front door of the wee cottage half an hour ago at seven pm on the dot, holding a bunch of pink hibiscus that he been in awe of, growing wild in the dry ditch at the end of the one long street. Eilidh had clapped her hands apparently tickled by his gesture when she answered the door.

'Depends?' She repeated then took her time before answering. 'Oh on muckle(1). . . *factors* ye might say.' Eilidh's words rose through and beyond its normally liltingly pleasing upward scale ending on a camp parody of the local accent as she began to get up from the sofa and to her feet, but she stumbled and reached to grab Walt's knee and steadied herself. 'Oops, these infernal feet. Sorry, Walter.'

Walt was as far from sorry as he felt he had ever been. His right knee still glowed wonderfully as he listened to Eilidh's business coming from her neat wee kitchen.

'Where are your manners, Eilidh McCrorie, my lass?. . .A wee dram while you wait, Walter. . . pre-prandial it is called is it not? Wash down that wine that you obviously dinnae care for,' Eilidh's deep throaty laugh added to Walt's attraction to this lovely lady as she added, 'Now I am getting to ken you, nae need for formal politeness, eh?'

Walt threw back the cloudy, yellow-tinged wine that he only sipped once. It had tasted peculiar. This was different! Wow! Eilidh caught him beaming as she came in with a bottle and two large glasses.

The Night Away…at last…mibbe

'Full bodied, aye, meant to be swallowed whole, I should have said. Would you like another or-', she held out one of the crystal tumblers.

'Whisky, please. Just a wee one.' Walt took the large glass from her. Their fingers touched lightly. Now his right hand tingled. It reminded him of his first touch of IT. The sensation could not be a warning, surely?

'*A wee one*? Now, that is a measure completely unknown to the entire village of Drumhumble. . .' She began to pour carefully. '*The Drumhumble One Year Old*'. Our maist mature, None of our cooking drams for a special guest. *Slainthe vas*, Walter.'

'Please call me Walt.' He said through the vinous glow that was now about to become golden, watching his glass too quickly fill.

There was a light, brief bark from outside.

Eilidh went to the back door, opened it and a black and white collie dog bounded past her and pulled up to bark excitedly in front of Walt. Eilidh came in hurriedly.

'Wheest! Wheest, Angus.' She patted the dog who sat immediately, panting with its long pink tongue lolling from side to side. 'This is Walt. Walt this is Angus. Now you have been introduced you can be friends.' She smiled at Walt, 'Angus has never met an Outsider.'

'What age is he, is Angus?'

'Oh . . .maybe. . . twenty-five.'

Eilidh's 'wee supper' had been superb: some kind of cheese-topped vegetable casserole that any meat would only have desecrated. It had helped soak up some of Walt's threatening stupor. He felt he would soon be as sound as Angus seemed to be, sprawled over Eilidh' fluffy slippers.

'Do you like wee cigars, Walt?' Eilidh opened a peculiar box revealing neatly packed, small thick cigars.

'I don't know. I can't remember. . .can't remember ever-'

'Well you are in for a treat. Drumhumble's finest. Home grown and cured – I rolled them myself, on my bare thighs. . .' she gave a deep chuckle.

Walt's imagination caused his hand to tremble as he took one of the two cigars Eilidh extracted from the strange box that he would later know as a humidor.

Eilidh's twinkling eyes hinted that she could have been teasing as she produced a match box and began her cigar ritual with the first long match, saying, 'Observe and learn master Wilson. One of many new things this dominie may teach you. . .'

'IT as you call it is what we locals call The Shield. It was, was *built* for want of the proper word in 1985. Thank goodness. I wasn't even a sparkle in my parents eyes but, God rest them, they told me that the Shield saved the village from some pestilence that erupted just the following year in what my books tell me was called the U.S.S.R And-'

'You mean the Chernobyl disaster?'

'Was that-'

'Did you not see the pictures on television?'

'Television? Oh, do you mean the moving pictures machine?' Oh, that was a complete failure in Drumhumble, apparently, again well before my time. This village is too *remote*. And too expensive apparently it would be to ensure a. . .a signal. So Gran. . .eh, so I was told.'

'But surely you would get the news on the radio?'

The Night Away…at last…mibbe

'Not after 1985. The Shield, remember? Some of the older villagers used to claim to miss their radios, mumping about the hellish interference. . .well it's true what they say that there is always something to pay for something that is really good. And that The Shield is. I cannot imagine being, living at the mercy of the weather. How uncivilised. . .downright barbaric!'

'But surely. . .well all these crops. . .you. . .well, everybody needs rain.' Walt thought back to that physical watershed when he had first hit IT - The Shield.

'Och, of course we do. But not every day like the bad old days that the old ones used to tell about but when they remembered the dismal dreary dreich times they stopped moaning about their radios no longer working.'

'But how do you, how does the rain get to the crops, to-'

'By opening it when we need it. And always at night.'

'So, it does open!'

'Silly man, of course. How else could you have got here?'

'And would the radios not work at night?'

'No, the hellish interference. . .was at night. And there was and is no signal at all when the Shield-'

'So, how, who. . .would this Granny Mulch. . .does she-?

'It is not for me to. . .you would have to ask her herself.'

'When can-'

'All in good time. Granny Mulch's good time.'

3.

THREEPLAY

    Eilidh was nervously excited. It was time. She was assessing herself in the small mirror on the cabinet, now checking her negligee. She hoped she had not overdone it, overdosed her beau with the whisky. She knew the Granny-sized potion in the Drumhumble Burgundy would be exact but the Drumhumble One Year Old was maybe too powerful for any Outsider, never mind a wee chappie like Walt. *I was just trying to mak siccar* she told herself and shuddered away a thought of the Frugal Fiasco.

No, this time, Granny and her magic potion would ensure it. When Walt woke up he would be instantly smitten, and fall in love with the first person he set eyes upon. Eilidh Isla McCrorie. Thereafter Nature would take its course. It was meant to be. *Two virgins together*, Granny had said. It was romantic. Eilidh could hardly wait but wait she must, Granny's warning that she must allow time for the potion to work. She must let Walt sleep until he wakened naturally. . .in an unnatural state.

    And he did.

    Eilidh found Walt and Angus in an unnatural embrace.

The dog was in distress, lightly whimpering but Walt seemed in heaven, a beatific smile on his face as he cuddled and caressed the collie whose confused eyes now appealed to his mistress for rescue.

4.

NO FOURPLAY

    '*Another* Cock-up!' Toby the cat was wakened from the Big Chair by Granny's shout. That nosy, chattering, cockatoo's silence confirmed this was serious.

The Night Away...at last...mibbe

'*Jist to mak siccar*, pah! Do you not trust Granny?! So ye fed him the One Year Old Special. To an Outsider?! Are ye mad, woman? He couldnae handle the The Inn's w*ater* when he arrived and you. . .Outsider's need time to *acclimatise*. Yer as daft as auld Adonald. . .Ye'll be telling me next I should include warnings about side effects with my potions. . .*will cause drowsiness*; *do not operate heavy machinery* and for pity's sake 'do not take along with 120 proof uisge-beatha.(2) And you the dominie. . .'

'I am truly sorry, Granny. . .what are we going to do?' Eilidh sobbed.

'*We*? You mean *me*. I have a good mind to. . .and stop greetin,' Granny sighed resignedly, visibly softening as she embraced Eilidh. 'I know, I know. . .two tries, two failures, but Granny will sort things.'

'Oh, thank you, Granny what would I. . .what would *Drumhumble* do without you?'

Granny released Eilidh a little but held both hands on Eilidh's shoulders and peered intently into her tear filled eyes. 'Who's been saying. . . ?'. Granny stopped and shook her head mumbling to herself as she turned her back on her patient, '*Get a hold of yerself, witch, the lass was just being nice. . .*'

Not for the first time she cursed her lack of omniscience. It was only with her Fergus she was able to know everything about him at all times. Up to now that had been enough for her to run her realm. As long as Fergus was completely in charge of the everyday things then through *her Fergus* Granny had the knowledge for total control of *her Drumhumble*. But Fergus wanted a phequing holiday. How was she-?

'When will the. . .infatuation wear off?' Eilidh interrupted Granny's other main worry.

'Usually about a week. But that's only if some eejit disnae mix ma *measured potion* wi' hooch! And ye cannae just cut a spell, just like that.

Normally.' Granny scratched her head. 'Everything ayeways happens at once. I need time tae think. . .'

But time was what she was too short of. She had promised her Fergus and she always kept her promises, well tried to, but how the green blazes was wally Walt going to be up to snuff to stand in for Fergus on his week's gallivant if he was mooning about with a collie dug?

Eilidh, Toby and Cocky watched Granny suddenly grab her coat from the back of the front door.

Granny was going 'out'! This was serious-*more than* serious. Granny *only* went out as far as Toby knew when there was a baby to be delivered, by *her deil*-livery or a cremation to perform. . .

Toby watched Granny turn at the door and bark at Eilidh, 'Where exactly are the two lovebirds?!'

'Ah dinna ken. When I came back from the toilet, they had gone. . .and so had Angus's lead.'

'They've eloped then.' Granny nodded and grunted, 'If anybody asks, tell them I've gone to see a man about his dog,' and disappeared though the front door.

Literally.

CHAPTER 10: GM v WWW...
catchweight and no-contest

1.

LIFT OFF

GRANNY WAS ENJOYING herself.

She still had it!

Good old necessity, not only the mother of invention, but capable of resurrecting long lost powers: powers she had been too scared to summon because she was sure she was 'past it'. Too old. . .too old, nothing!

Bejeessus it was good to be oot.

It was a damned sight better to FLY!

Again. And no sign of a befuddling blinding migraine. She would think about that later. . .if she remembered. . .

She swooped low over all the nearest, tallest crops where the man and dog would be hardest to spot, too easy to hide in the corn or the tobacco even the hops but there was no sign of them. She decided to test her rapid-soaring power now that she was warmed up seeking a witch's eye view. Badness, this felt good. . .again. . .now for the old vertical climb. . .Wheeeee!

'Ouch! Ya bugger ye! She held her throbbing head. The bluidy Shield! She had soared too high. She had forgotten about the Shield. *Forgot* about the Scutum *again*. She shrugged off the ever-encroaching fear of her demise. . .she couldn't be past it if she could still fly, surely?

When had she last gone for even a pleasure flight? Certainly before 1985-before she created the Shield. . .now she remembered.

The Hinderberg. 1937. It's last flight, she shuddered at the sudden previously repressed memory but again began rationalising away the guilt about her puncturing the leviathan airship when she crashed into it as it sailed over her domain. It was on its way from Frankfurt to its final conflagration trying to dock in a field in America. *That teeny wee hole I made had nothing to do with. . . anything. Anyway, naebody noticed. . .and they are <u>still</u> arguing about what caused the disaster. It <u>might</u> have been sabotage or a static spark or lightning or incendiary paint or. . .*but she was kidding herself, she *knew* it was a *puncture* that started things and the hydrogen and fuel leaks theories were correct but they didn't identify the primary cause – a witch oot oan a joy ride that went oot o' control. . .

And she had never flown since. But this was an emergency only she could fix. . .

She circled her domain for the second time, painfully mindful of the Shield's severe height restriction but again relishing the joy of rediscovering her power of flight.

'Broomsticks are for beginners' -she thought back, nearly five hundred years when she was able to discard her witch's 'L' plates and the broomstick 'trainer' (like the wee safety wheels on a learner's bicycle) but her cackling lessened with the surfacing of the deep and certain knowledge that this would be her last flight.

She could still see Ben Her and its permanent snow caps just outside the scope of her *Scutum* but she knew her eyesight was not what it used to be - damn it, all what it *should* be - and all the potions she had mixed and drunk had failed. Her eyesight like her memory lapses were yet more evidence of her declining powers. In her hey days, or even shorter, say a couple of hundred years back she would have spotted them by now, both man and dog.

2.

VIRGIN MAN'S BEST FRIEND

Literally and emotionally Walt was head over heels. He had tripped on Angus's lead again as they had begun the climb up the first foothill towards Ben Her.

They lay side by side resting, both panting. The dog began licking his new master's face. Walt beamed. It was reciprocal now. Angus was in love with *him*!

At first it had been a drag, hauling Angus out of the cottage but it was worth the effort of overcoming his lovely collie's initial resistance, its planking his bottom and digging its back feet in, but Walt felt his overwhelming love for this beautiful dog had now won the day. Gradually Angus had stopped whimpering, eventually trotting freely by Walt' side as they had run for the hills.

Walt licked Angus as Angus licked Walt. The cliché about 'Man's best friend being his dog' came to his mind. Well, cliches were also ' only *truths* told once too often'. And it was true! Walt vaguely remembered some stupid obsession that had once possessed him about not ever having a girlfriend, but like other recent increasingly infrequent attempts he had made to remember his past it remained fuzzy, out of reach. Anyway, it was completely *inconsequential* now that he had Angus!

It was time to put Angus's love to the test...

    Time to unleash his love.

3.

IT'S A KNOCKOUT

With little warning Granny all of a sudden felt worn out. Knackered. That one soar and the bang on the head didnae help. . .

But, now close to the eastern boundary of the Shield, she spotted them lying, cuddling on the grassy foothill. Basking and canoodling in the sun. Time to put an abrupt end to-

Crash! Granny landed with a bump on her rump. In her excited glee at finally spotting the pair she had forgotten how to perform neither an emergency stop nor a controlled landing.

Luckily Walter's thick head had softened her landing.

She had knocked him out. Good. Save her time later. The painful shock should bring him back to his senses. . .once he recovered them. *If he ever had any* she snorted.

Now for the pathetic dog. Granny didn't like dogs, give her cats every time (even birds). . . as for this typical, stupid, drooling, yapping, frightened mutt. . .she picked up the lead lying beside Walt's unconscious hand and whipped a crack out of it.

'Home! Now!!' A shocked but relieved Angus stopped his frightened barking and scooted down the gentle slopes, his black tail rising all the while from between his black and white legs, now wagging, it and himself, back to normal.

Granny peched and panted as she heaved a limp comatose Walt to his feet, praying for lift off and regretting the absence of a turbo-charged broomstick.

But the effort cost her the last of her strength.

She sagged, her knees buckling as she crumpled to the lush grass and joined Walt in unconsciousness.

CHAPTER 11: ANIMAL (and bird) RESCUE

1.

Cat Flap v Bird Cage

TOBY THE CAT woke with a start to the frantic squawking of Cocky the cockatoo.

But it wasn't the bird that had wakened the cat. It was Granny. She was in trouble. Toby knew. Familiars just did. Toby scooted to the cat flap, turned, arched his back and hissed at the bird flapping, amok in its cage.

'Fat lot of use you are in an emergency!'

'I can help, I can help. Let me oot, let me oot!' Cocky screeched.

Something in Toby caused him to pause, his right paw on the flap. 'How can you?-'

'Birds eye view. Birds eye-'

'Okay, okay, nae need tae repeat everything. . .I get it. I get. . . Yer no' talking to a birdbrain.' Toby scrambled, and sprachled up on to the tallboy that held the cage. His paw flicked furiously at the complicated clasp, that was too complex for brainless birds but not for clever cats, surely. The lock sprung and the cage door swung open.

Cocky shot up his ladder and cowered on her top perch.

'Ye think I am going to eat you?' Toby scoffed. 'If I wanted to eat you I would have done it ten years back, when ye were at least edible and no' a scrawny shilpit excuse for a plump-'

Cocky frantically hopped down the ladder and past a startled cat and flew aimlessly around the room, discarding a few feathers as she crashed into the window.

'Time to go. Time to-' the stunned bird mumbled.

'Okay, okay' Toby got his nascent schadenfreude under control, stifled a laugh, ran back to the door's cat flap and held it open for the bird.

'After you.' Toby watched the cockatoo stagger and waddle through the cat flap as his thoughts about scrawniness being sometimes useful were suddenly swept aside by: *'How the green blazes does Cocky ken about Granny? Had that bird acquired the powers of a proper familiar? Fourteen years cooped up with Granny Mulch might just do that. . .*

Eventually.

And the bloody bird was awake and squawking the alarm before me. . .

Toby could not and would not live with being anything less than Number One Familiar to Granny Mulch.

2.

The hills are alive.

'Here they are! Here they are!' a sunlit Cocky was hovering like a hawk over its intended prey.

The bluidy bird was first again. If Toby hadn't been so worried about Granny he would do something about Cocky the too-cocky cockatoo. But that could wait. The bird had found Granny. The tired cat sighed at both the thought of how insufferable the bird would be now with her feat and the ache in his back legs and paws as he began the climb.

'What kept you?! 'What kept-'

Animal (and bird) Rescue

'Shut it!' Toby gasped with what felt like his last breath. He was too old for treks like this.

The cat surveyed the twinned human wreckage as the bird gratefully landed beside the old woman and the young man. Cocky was also tired, unused to any flight beyond the internal confines of Granny's cottage.

'What to do? What to-'

'Oot the road.' Toby suddenly pawed Cocky aside, muttering 'Ye've served yer purpose, bird.' The cat felt the delightful frisson of actually laying a paw on the bird for the first time. Toby noted the flutter of white wings as the bird hopped aside hoping the too-cocky Cocky was enjoying a frisson too: a bad frisson- a Frisson of Shades of Things to Come.

A happier cat carefully approached Granny wondering if there was significance in the fact that she had her arm protectively across the chest of the unconscious stranger as they lay side by side, out to this world.

What had happened here? But more to the immediate point, 'What to do', right enough. . .? It would be night soon and the Shield would be opening way up here to allow the Outside rain to replenish the burns and let Nature retake both normal and irrigated courses.

And Granny would get wet. Not good at her age. If she was alive that is. . .

Toby prowled around the two unconscious forms, Cocky hopping and fluttering well out the way for safety and to allow the cat quiet to make its decision.

3.

If it smells like it and tastes like it...

Walt woke wiping his face and automatically flailing his arms to remove whatever was sitting on his face. Whatever it was it had woken him with. . .something warm and. . .Ye gods, it was a cat, a large black cat and this was. . .he wiped his hand over his tingling damp cheeks. . .the bloody cat had pissed on him! The stink was awful, the slightest of inadvertent tastes confirmed it. Walt tried to stand to kick the cat but he felt pinned by someone's arm encased in a puce coloured sleeve.

He managed to scramble from under the arm, all the while eyeing the cat that eyed him back. Walt thought better of assaulting this enormous cat when. . .

'He's alive! He's alive!'

Toby wanted to shut the bird up, regretting again his inability to talk in the presence of normal humans and settled for silent murder instead.

Cocky easily avoided the cat's rush with a swift take-off and hovered safely, enough feet in the air.

Walt had not a clue what was going on and what had happened to him. A pissing cat and a squawking cockatoo and a prostrate body; Walt's eyes darted back and forth and upwards. He remembered something about a collie dog and then something cracking down on his head.

He held his head and looked at the cat, the bird and the body. He remembered enough to know that it was something *heavy* that had landed on him. That left out the scrawny looking bird and the evil staring cat -- big as it was – so it must be. . .no way! How could, what looked like a woman. . .an *old* woman. . .a *very* old woman suddenly land on him? Out of the blue? C'mon. . .

Animal (and bird) Rescue

The cat started miaowing loudly. The bird screeched:

'Help Granny! Help Granny!'

Walt gently rolled the woman over fully revealing her face. She wasn't old, she was *ancient*! And she was GREEN!

How could she have. . .but this re-wondering was shattered by the combined cacophony of the cat's yowl and the bird's screech.

'That's the way to do it! That's the way to do it!' Help Granny! Help Granny!'

Granny? Granny? Was this the Granny Mulch he had heard about in the 'courtroom'. . .and hinted at by Eilidh?

He must have thought out loud: the screech confirmed it.

'Granny Mulch! Granny Mulch!'

The loud purr of the cat seemed to confirm Walt's discovery and it appeared friendly now, no longer malevolent, as it approached Walt, the purr so loud, so strong Walt felt the vibration against his trouser leg as the cat rubbed against it, arching it back.

One question answered apparently, so now he knew who it was that had somehow landed on him, but that didn't help with the questions of how she got here and what to do with her.

The bird and the cat seemed to be hinting, literally pointing him in the right direction as they in silent concert flew and ran a little back and forth indicating he should return all the way back to Drumhumble.

But should he leave her and go for help? Or. . .

4.

It's along way to tote a Granny

He would have to put her down. She might be ancient bent and small but she was solid. Solid bone.

His bent back and rounded shoulders ached from the unconscious body they now toted fireman style; his numbed arms had given up carrying their load ages ago. He laid her on the grass.

It was almost dark. They had reached the level grounds having just descended the last of the foothill. He could see the green smoke from the chimney in the village. *Green?! The smoke-*

'Need to hurry! Need to hurry! The white bird commanded, the black cat miaowed loudly in seeming agreement. Walt sighed and prepared to lift Granny Mulch again but she seemed to stir as he propped her against his shoulder. He gently laid her back down as she came to groaning and mumbling.

'Granny Mulch? Granny are you–'Walt began to ask softly.

The old woman scrambled to her feet remarkably quickly.

'Right as rain. Before you ask. And we better be quick before it soaks us. . .Walter.'

Walt, mouth agape, eventually trotted to catch up with the flying bird, the running cat and the purposefully striding ancient woman. The ancient *green* woman.

CHAPTER 12: ALL IS REVEALED
(nearly)

1.

One small step

'In ye come. Dinnae jist staun there like a spare thingummy at a thingy,' Granny ordered Walt then barked, 'Wipe yer feet first!'

Walt obeyed reluctantly, but he felt sure he must enter if he wanted to find out more about his place in the village of Drumhumble – this was more than instinct, a stronger sensation altogether, something new. And alien. But something he '*kent*' he must face if he was ever to escape.

He felt he had done more than enough in ensuring that Granny Mulch had returned to what he assumed was her home – a large thatched roofed cottage at the end of a lane well back from the village street; a creepy cottage that even Hansel and Gretel would have had the good sense to run from. The green smoke from the bent chimney would have been deterrent enough.

He plucked the briar, bramble and other strange and unknown detritus that had clung to his borrowed woollen shirt coming up through the overgrown lane; plants that appeared more than just alive, reaching out to refuse his progress.

Walt gave himself a final brush down, wiped his feet on the huge doormat that overlapped the small doorstep and entered the cottage.

2.

Say it again Tam.

One of Frugal McDougall's too few true pleasures in his too busy life was watching somebody else being good at their job while he himself took a break. And the only Drummer Frugal rated was his mate Tam. Tam McKee, blacksmith.

Frugal was in the smiddy, perched on a wall bench watching Tam expertly multi-task, his foot pumping the wee back bellows that roared up the furnace to allow the blacksmith the right temperature to free both hands to intricately forge a repair or replacement for some long agricultural-looking hand tool that Frugal hadn't a clue, and couldn't care less, about.

Frugal was nervous, waiting for Tam to finish for the day. He always came last thing when Tam's latest apprentice and his trained journeyman had both been released for the day and the weekend. This was Friday.

Tam and Frugal Time.

Tam always kept the most difficult tasks back to concentrate for this last hour or so. He didn't mind Frugal's presence as long as he kept his mouth shut until he was finished.

To stay his sudden impatience Frugal lit a wee cigar, its smoke no competition for the ever-present fug in the busy smiddy that he gazed through, not really taking in Tam's delicate frenetic touches to the unknown implement.

Frugal's well of curiosity was full right now and had been filling for some time with bigger issues than furrowing fermer repairs. That's why he had come: today was more than their Friday tea, dram and 'men talk.' Frugal's only men talk – talking *at* Adonald provided nothing in return and as for this new Wally, geez, he had him more scared than the auld man and had deliberately cut short the wee

All is Revealed (nearly)

eedjit's inappropriate questions, the last of Granny's potion working its magic by playing havoc with the wee runt's memory.

Tam McKee swept the tongs through ninety degrees and deftly deposited the orange-red glowing whatever in the huge water bucket, the violent hiss of clashing temperatures drowning his opening remarks to Frugal.

Frugal anticipated them. He knew what Tam would say when he had told him of his plans last week but a perverse force (and he had plenty of those) had brought him here. Tam had said nothing by way of response, saying only that he 'wid gie it a mickle thocht' and that he would respond this Friday. Today.

Frugal needed to hear Tam's predictable objections out loud to stiffen his resolve, because he was starting to get cold feet about going Outside. On *holiday*.

Tam wiped his hands on a dirty rag and reached for the two big well-worn tea mugs and held one up in his right hand.

'Says it all. Got your name on it, Fergus. Mug.'

Tam as ever, the man of few words, turned his back on Frugal, and began busying himself making their weekly strong tea.

Tam had never said much: from when, as wee boys out playing, to sitting side by side all the way through school, through Tam's apprenticeship then as the second in command journeyman here in the smiddy, then *the* blacksmith once the auld pompous prick McClachlan passed on at 75.

And here they were, both aged 50. One single and discontent the other married, with two kids, the dochter pregnant and about to make him a grandpa. Tam couldn't wait and he was already *content*. He gruffed the word at Frugal.

'*Content*. Ye should try it sometime, Fergus.' Tam handed over Frugal's mug of tea and Frugal added the customary compulsory complimentary splash of uisge-beath to both teas from the bottle he always brought – a bottle that they always finished once a week, every Friday.

This was what Frugal had come for: a tongue lashing from Tam in his pal's own inimitable laconic style. The more Tam decried Frugal's 'plan', the more Frugal felt he would justify it to himself, at worst it would force him to really think through what was at best still a vague but powerful impulse.

To Frugal, maybe a friend's scorn was just what he wanted. Exactly what he needed right this minute.

Bring it on… say it again Tam!

3

questions – not wishes.

Toby was in his basket carefully watching the caged bird checking for any prescience, any powers that Toby himself did not possess. Did the bird ken before Toby what Granny was up to? But the cockatoo was silent staring down from its perch, seemingly afraid of the Outsider but most importantly seemingly as ignorant as Toby felt. This was the first of Them either bird or cat had seen. And the Outsider was right here in Granny's kitchen in the Big Chair, a virtual guest of honour, now listening to Granny who was speaking in that accent she slipped into only when she was vexed or angry. But she was far from angry; she seemed fully recovered from her ordeal and back in control doing what she did best.

Controlling.

Her *raison d'etre*.

All is Revealed (nearly)

'. . .so, it behoves me young Walter, for your assistance today. . . mind you I would have managed myself. . .eventually. . .so, instead of the traditional three wishes I shall grant you three questions. Yes!' Granny clapped her hands as if she had all of a sudden come to a decision. 'Yes, that seems appropriate. . .and fair. Apposite. Just. Yes, Walter you may ask three questions. . .and I promise I shall answer them truthfully. All three.'

Walt panicked. He had so *many* questions! And this crone was *granting* him only three. . .who did she think she was, some kind of witch? *Time to man up, Walt,* he told himself. That bang on the head – however she had accomplished it – ironically seemed to have *restored* some of his memory of times *before*. . .*before he had come to in that dingy back room of his 'workplace' in this queer village with its queerer villagers* – so he wouldn't be wasting any of his *three* questions on banalities like 'name rank and serial number'. Oh no! he suddenly knew who he was, where he came from – the curious, incongruous Norfolk accent the ancient woman was using maybe had acted as another sharp prompt . . .
'How do you know my name and-' Walt's involuntary blurt was cut short.
'*One question at a time*' Granny sang to the tune of *'One Day at a Time (sweet Jesus).* How do I know that you are called Walter Wilson Winston? Is that your first question?' Granny sounded like that quiz show host (with a Norfolk twang)
'I suppose so.' Walt conceded.
'Well, it is, no supposing about it and no changing your mind, that's the rules!'
'Who says so?'
'Nicola Mulch aka Granny Mulch. And that is your second question answered. Now, do you want your third question now or shall I answer your first question, firstly, Walter Wilson Winston?'

The Granny State of Drumhumble

So much for manning up and taking control. . .Walt realised he was up against not just some daft old woman, but a sharp smart one. He would need to be wary if he was to learn at least some, now down to *one* of the plethora of things he wanted to know. . . some, of immediate past, not a few about the present, but most, importantly about the future.

Worries had already begun forming about neglecting his business by being seemingly trapped beyond the back of beyond in the middle of nowhere. After all she *might* just be a witch. He would have asked her, but he only had one question left.

'Well?' Granny prompted and gave an enigmatic grin. Or was it a disguise for a knowing smirk?

Walt looked around looking for inspiration at the jars and earthenware containers of all sizes and shapes that lined the shelves on all four walls and seemed to have overspilled onto the cluttered broad wooden table in front of him. He was aware of the two creatures watching him closely, wondering if the caged bird and the basketed cat were as interested in him as they looked. Did they really want to know as much as Walt did? Or did they *ken* already?

 'The answer to my first question. . .please. . .Ms Mulch.'

'What was it again? And you call me Granny. Certainly not Ms. . .I'm Granny or GM, like everybody else calls me. . .Walter. . .or Walt as I ken you like to be called. . .oh aye, how is it that I ken your name? Well. . .the answer is. Research.' Granny paused.

Walt didn't understand but just caught himself. . .or so he thought
'How-?
'Well, now-'
'No. Stop!' I didn't finish my question. Walt rubbed his flushed face. This was a nightmare. He must leap to the chase.
'How do I get out of here, no not *here*! but the village?!'
'Not possible at present I am afraid. . . but you and I shall come to an arrangement. And that's your third and final answer.'

All is Revealed (nearly)

The quiz show was over.

4.
Tam plays a blinder and a trump.

Frugal's usual smugness was back. He had managed to bat aside all Tam's objections about the 'sense' and practicalities of going Outside for a 'holiday'. Tam reached for the bottle and poured the last of the Drumhumble six month old malt, their favourite quaffing spirit. It had taken them much longer than their usual time to finish it. Tam had never talked so much, obviously having really thought about Frugal's 'holiday' plan over the last week.

But Frugal had cheated, lied (both second nature to him) claiming that it was simply curiosity that motivated him, and that he simply wanted to experience Outside 'just the once before he was too old to enjoy it'. He said nothing about trying to find his mother, never mind his father. He was cunning enough to reckon Tam's devil's advocate objections to that real reason might just overwhelm his resolve.

But Tam had saved his last obstacle for the last. It was a big hurdle to Frugal's plan. The biggest.

Frugal sipped his whisky and listened with mounting dismay.

'We'll imagine Granny keeps her word and lets you out and away on this *holiday*. What are you. . .how are you. . . what about '*money*'?' Tam asked, his voice rising a half octave higher than its usual profundo,
'Money?' Frugal asked.
'Aye. I believe that is what they call it, what they use Outside. Ye'll need to get your hands on some of that. Unless yer plan includes *humphing* ample provisions and enough claithes tae sleep rough for a week, ye'll need tae pay for bed and board, not to mention all the other tempting *novelties and curiosities* yer over-enquiring mind might seek out. . . ye'll need to *pay* for them. How are ye going tae manage without the appropriate *currency*?'

The Granny State of Drumhumble

'I'm beginning tae wish I hadnae telt ye-'

'Was it wishful or fanciful thinking or did ye just overlook the hard fact that this village has not had a common currency with the Outside since before either of us was hatched, Fergus?'

Frugal hadn't really considered the fact that Drumhumble's medium of financial exchange- that topped up the much used barter system -- the tokens that he himself regulated as boss of the company store -- would probably not pass Outside for *currency*.
Luckily Frugal was on a roll, his previous successful deception and the whisky combined. . .*Inspired Desperation* was better than Necessity and he knew instantly the answer lay as ever with Granny.
With Granny's gold reserves. The many left-over nuggets she had hoarded from the Helmsdale mid nineteenth century gold rush.
But he couldn't tell Tam. Granny would kill him. Certainly give the holiday a knock back. For good.
'I'll think of something.' he dissembled.

Tam shook his head in mock despair as Frugal raised his last glass in toast.

'Slainthe,   Tam,   thanks   for   all   your   help.'

CHAPTER 13: SECOND CHANCES AND MORE REVELATIONS

1.

Like Xmas Eve

WEEKS LATER, WALT was a lot less tired and much leaner and stronger. But only a little wiser. The healthy food and the hard manual work had wrought his pleasing physical change and gradually he began to remember bits and pieces of driving north from Norfolk to. . .to wherever this was.

And he had 'met' the notorious and feared Granny Mulch. And survived. Her parting words played again in his head as he shuffled the full and empty casks in the cellar. Thankfully on his own.

'Thank you again, I'll be in touch, Walter. Just after *All Eedjits Day.*'

He wanted to find out about this apparently significant event in the village calendar and had steeled himself to ask Boss Frugal, but strangely the innkeeper all week had looked permanently preoccupied, unusually nervous, twitching at the smallest sound and Walt had settled for enjoying the break from the usual bullying harassment and creepy invasion of his personal space.

Walt had asked Adonald earlier in the week but had been met with a chackling 'Ye'll find oot soon enough. If I telt ye widnae believe me. . .but see me? ah canna wait'.

And every day Adonald had given him a reminder, a parodied singing countdown, his glee rising with each passing day, like a kid in the interminable few days before Christmas.

And this was 'Xmas Eve', All Eedjits Day was tomorrow.

Walt could hear Adonald's tread in the bar above singing his medley. He was sure Adonald was practicing for the Big Day. Walt felt sure Adonald would be performing.

Tomorrow.

The reedy but pure voice penetrated the ancient timbers. Walt knew it was a parody of *'Save the Last Dance for me'*.

'Jist remember who's carrying ye hame
And ower whae's back yer gonnae be
So darlin', save the last cans for me...'

2.

A woman's gotta do what…

Eilidh was nervous despite Granny's assurances that on All Eedjits Eve Frugal would be busy 'negotiating for money' at Granny's and Adonald would be sound in his bunk in the inn's lean-to, resting for his performance the next day.

She dabbed the powerfully fragrant apparently unperfumed 'perfume' Granny had quickly made in front of her as she crushed the petals of an admixture of bright flowers and seeds mostly unknown to Eilidh. Granny had muttered some portentous words and with remarkable speed produced a small bottle of blackish green liquid, poured it over the crushed flowers resting in a small bowl. There had been an instant reaction of hiss and bubble quickly followed by purple vapour. Granny had seemed satisfied, ignoring the squawk and miaow of her bird and cat, she had carefully poured the resultant brew into an empty phial and handed it to Eilidh with the words:

'This will be potent for only three days. No more than two dabs behind each ear and nowhere else, or else. . .and make sure our

Second Chances and More Revelations

Walter caws canny with the hooch this time. . .this is powerful stuff. With this, plus your natural feminine charms and no' bad looks, you'll have him in your virgin's bed in less time than it takes to skin a dragon.'

Eilidh carefully took the phial from the drawer in her compact dresser, gingerly removed the neat cork stopper tentatively sniffing the contents. As Granny had claimed, Eilidh smelled nothing. The scent only worked on men, affecting their testosterone. She tilted some of the lightly opaque purplish liquid on to her index finger and dabbed twice behind each ear. As she replaced the stopper a tingle began to grow behind both her ears. The tingle became a glow circling and suffusing her head that seemed to calm her nerves and fire her determination. She began to look forward to the challenge ahead, but her confidence received a dent as she now remembered the witch's valedictory words when closing Granny's cottage door.

'For any sake dinnae let him touch the water tap on the bar counter. He nearly died the last time. . .and leave that blasted dug o' yours at hame in his kennel!'

It was a starlit night. Eilidh stepped out into the empty street. Most folk would be having an early night with some others still busy preparing indoors for the predawn start of All Eedjits Day.

She had reached the inn and was standing outside. She listened for any sign of life thinking of Granny's certainty that the 'wee something' Granny had rubbed into Water's head bump -- telling him it would reduce the swelling -- had completely wiped all traces of meeting Eilidh or "that faithless, frolicking, phequing collie" from his memory. 'It'll be like meeting you for the first time. Go for it lass, third time lucky!'

Despite herself, she shuddered again at the Frugal fiasco and now the Angus one. . .third time indeed. And her last chance. . .

Pregnancy here I come she vowed and forcefully pushed at the inn's front door.

It was locked.

3.

A night to forget to remember

There was a rattle from the inn's front door. Walt turned from drying his last tumbler and placed it beside the others under the small gantry. Thankfully there had been hardly any customers all evening and the last two had staggered out under Frugal's arms. Frugal had left with them and ordered Walt to lock up behind him, telling Walt to get "a good night's sleep because ye'll need all yer strength and what wits ye have for tomorrow, Wally boy.'"

This was virtually the first words Frugal had spoken to him for a few days now. Even the sarcasm he had just used was subdued. Something was definitely worrying him. Walt was glad, almost enjoying the mundane tasks he now performed without the close supervision and closer physical presence.

A kind of freedom.

There was now a knock at the door. Three gentle raps. Probably one or both of the last two drunks back for their denied 'swift wee one for the road'. Walt ignored them. Just as they had ignored all attempts by Walt all evening to engage them in conversation. Just like all his other customers since he had started serving behind the bar. None of them would have anything to do with Walt other than over-politely, tersely place orders for their strong drink. It seemed to him more than suspicion of Outsiders, more as if they were under orders to tell him nothing.

The knock was louder more insistent, sounding desperate, continuing.

'Go away! We're closed!'

'Please let me in. I do not want serving. Well I…'

A giggle. . .a *female* voice! Walt had never seen a woman in the inn. It had been 'men only'. Only sour silent surly men.

What did this. . .*she* want?

As if answering his thought, she spoke again, her voice whispering. Walt put his ear to the ancient thick oaken door and caught some of her words…

'. . .and answer. . .you must have. . .questions. . .Granny asked me. . .'

Walt quickly turned the large key still in post and hauled the door open through all of the protesting creaks.

A hooded figure was framed in a backdrop of moonlight, her features unidentifiable, but the shape was definitely feminine and the clincher was the scent that wafted in bringing Walt to his knees.

Literally.

4.

The woman chooses

Eilidh helped Walt to his feet. Worrying that her perfume potion had overworked even from a distance; she checked his face at arms length, a hand on each of his shoulders. He looked as if he was in a blissful dwam(1). Remembering Granny's warning, she led him to the booth in the farthest corner from the bar and its forbidden water spigot.

Eilidh had not been in here since the start of the Frugal Fiasco that had reached its anti-climax back at her cottage. She shuddered trying to suppress the horrid memory as she gently lowered Walt onto a bare wooden seat, part of a snug booth for two.

Walt recovered to find himself looking across the narrow table at the most beautiful woman he had ever seen. She wore a red dress that revealed the most fascinating alluring shoulders. He noticed the hooded cloak discarded beside her on the bench seat and suddenly remembered he had opened the door to her and. . .

'So, you are with us once more, Walter. . .' her voice was soft and lilting, he wasn't surprised. She was *perfect*.

'Granny sent me. Granny Mulch', she smiled. 'Och I'm forgetting my manners, I'll be being drummed out of Drumhumble for my lack of *hospitality*', she laughed, tossing her head and revealing gorgeous teeth. 'I'm Eilidh. Eilidh McCrorie. I'm the Drumhumble dominie. The teacher.' She reached across the table and took Walt's limp hand.

Her hand felt amazingly soft, just wonderful. Now she was squeezing his gently as she performed a handshake that Walt didn't want to end. Ever.

He eventually recovered enough to go to the bar to pour them each a drink.

Eilidh had ordered beer and thankfully Walt had decided on the same avoiding the possible calamity of him adding *any* water to a dram from that spigot.

She thought things were going to plan, he obviously did not remember her, just as Granny had promised. She took the pint from Walt reminding herself that it was 7% proof and was aptly labelled *Drumhumble Durler*. Powerful and perhaps not to be mixed with whatever Granny had had her lodge behind her ears. What was it that English bard had claimed – '*Increasing the desire but ruining the performance*? She should speed things up, take his mind off the beer. . .starting with leaving her hand on Walt's as he tried to transfer the glass. She bent forward as well, hopefully releasing more pheromones or whatever Granny had conjured up for her.

It worked: she could see it in his shy eyes. He was besotted. Now softly, softly, Eilidh.

' I am here to answer any questions you have, Walter. Granny is feeling a wee bit guilty – it is not like her I can assure you. You must be special indeed Mr Walter Wilson Winston – anyway she sent me to, as she said, *'properly* answer any-'

But right now, Walt had only one question. And it was a BIG one, but he dare not ask it. Virgin or not he had enough instinct to tell him that a gentleman did not do that and if the growth in his woollen breeks continued it would soon be choking enough to preventing him asking any questions at all.

It is said that 'a standing cock has no conscience'.

It is also deaf and dumb,

5.

Pillow Talk.

They were in bed. Eilidh's bed.

Walt had little idea how he had got here. He had a vague memory of an intoxicating aroma and strangely of locking the door of the inn from the outside, he reached down to his heap of clothes. The large ancient key was easily confirmed – he didn't want to waste any questions on mundane items. . . Oh no.

Eilidh had promised to answer all his questions *after*.

Well, it was now *twice* 'after'. It was *Question Time* but would it be *Answer Time* and would he obtain the *Big Answer*?

The Granny State of Drumhumble

How to get out of here?

Escape from Drumhumble.

He could feel her soft hand on his belly and the cobra began to rise under the soothing words of the charmer. Again. . .

Third time lucky, Eilidh remembered Granny's valedictory words. The first time had been almost premature; the second a BIG improvement, and by the feel of things this third time would do the trick.

Escape? Walt would have had difficulty spelling the word far less thinking about its meaning as in the flickers of the sweet-smelling candles, with increasing wonder he watched this loveliest of ladies elegantly straddle him.

Would the sex never end? Now *that* was an important question. Forget the trivial. . .whatever was on that stupid list of inane questions that had begun again to, no! *Used* to occupy his every thought. . .

Oooh. . .she released him. What now?

'This way now, my sweet Walter.' She kissed him softly, rolling over to lie face down next to him.

He knew this was called 'doggy-fashion' and it felt even better. Masterful. . .

Live for the moment, Walt! Tomorrow's another day. . .

But it was 'All Eedjits Day'. . .

The clock struck midnight and as if on cue a dog scrambled up on the bed and barked furiously in Walt's right ear, trying to burrow between their naked bodies, now licking its mistress's neck, then snarling in Walt's face.

Walt did not remember Eilidh's pet, but the collie dog remembered the treacherous human who once professed his love for him. . .Congreve's *woman scorned* is nothing compared to a dog rejected then replaced by its mistress.

Eididh knew she had boobed again, twice: thinking Angus was completely back to normal and that his kennel was secure.

'Down Angus! Down boy!' she ordered.

Both dog and boy obeyed.

Instantly.

6.

It's not so good to talk.

They lay in bed smoking. Walt was not a smoker, but these Drumhumble cigarillos Eilidh claimed to be 'home- made' were wonderfully satisfying -- a restorative closure to the frantic sexual activity.

A night of firsts: sex, cigarillos and love. And the greatest of these was love. Walt was in love, totally in love, but it was exhausting.

'I don't know what got into Angus, Walter. He's usually so friendly.' Eilidh tested her disingenuous claim.

'He maybe thought I was attacking you.'

'I know *you* were attacking me. . . *big* boy.' She was relieved. He really didn't remember.

They laughed. They cuddled. They slept.

But only briefly. Eilidh was out of bed, rummaging in her dresser. It woke Walt. He watched her naked form lit by the one bedside lamp. He could not believe it possible that this voluptuous woman could be in love with him. Surely, she could not be experiencing the same emotions as him? As well as the all-consuming passion, she made him feel, despite this niggling doubt, *worthy*. She had given him confidence in himself. Confident enough to question?

'Eilidh-' he began.

She turned, a little startled and gave him that smile. 'Sorry did I wake you, Walter. I'm just looking out my oldest clothes for today.'

'Oldest?'

'Oh, you'll see. I would not want to spoil the nice surprise.'

Second Chances and More Revelations

But that was the last question he would ask for a wee while. He watched her dab something behind each ear from a small bottle she replaced on the dresser then slink slowly towards the bed. The perfume beat her to it. Walt swooned, almost completely under the senses of sight and smell.

'Now where were we before Angus so, so rudely-' she covered him in kisses and fully enveloped him in that heavenly scent.

But the questions started again over a delicious breakfast of fruit salad, cheese and toast.

Some of the fruits were strange to him, Eilidh told him that they were all Drumhumble-grown: guava, papaya, mango, kiwi fruit, pineapple as well as the more commonplace peaches, apricots, plums apples, pears, strawberries and raspberries. It was accompanied by toasted home- made bread with indigenous creamy butter and delicious cheeses, all washed down with fresh coffee made from local beans. . .! Walt had to ask.

'Surely not?'

'You don't believe me?' Eilidh's surprise seemed genuine.

Where was he? Surely NOT in Scotland. . .?

And that started the deluge of questions. They poured out of him: where; when; who; why and most importantly HOW?

'Whoah, whoah, one question at a time, sweet Walter.'

'Sorry, Eilidh, I have so many.'

'Have to hurry you, Walt,' she looked at the tiny grandfather-like clock. ' I am due in the Left Field in twenty minutes. We can talk at lunch. Back here', she added smiling, raising a provocative eyebrow before beginning to clear the breakfast dishes.

'The Left Field?' he asked as she carried the empty plates into her wee kitchen.

The dog barked -- Walt hoped from outside and in its kennel.

'Naughty Angus, nothing for you! What was that, Walter? '

'The field, The left-?'

'The Left Field is where we hold Daft Eedjits Day. I am one of the many stars on today's bill', she added with a laugh.

Walt knew he would have to wait for his answers until after he had performed. . . again.

Despite being filled with the delicious breakfast it was more than curiosity that whetted his appetite for lunch.

CHAPTER 14: EEDJITS DAY

It had lived up to both the warnings and the promises.

The Daft Eedjits had been at it since before daybreak apparently. To Walt, it seemed the theme was a weird admixture of sport and revenge all enacted in the Left Field, which was more than large enough to accommodate all the villagers and their activities. Eilidh had told him that everybody, all of Drumhumble, would be here. Walt reckoned that there was well over two hundred people, all ages, from babies to adults as old as Adonald.

The babies had arrived in bespoke wooden carts which had initially served as conventional conveyancing prams but here in the Left Field they were re- employed as chariots in a crazy version of jousting. The babies, safely in a parent's arms, were replaced by an older kid in the cart holding a long wooden 'weapon', the end daubed in a cow pat, being pushed at a rival; the cleaner one at the end being declared the victor.

The sun shone warming the scene from its cobalt pure sky. Adonald himself could be seen mixing excitedly with a small group of men his own age.

The only one missing seemed to be Granny Mulch.

Walt had missed the early 'events' as Eilidh and he had lain in, exhausted with the bedroom gymnastics. Walt had loved every second and this novel afterglow was almost more pleasurable. The frantic activities he now viewed made no sense and held only little interest as his mind and emotions were elsewhere.

It was wonderful being in love. So this was *head over heels*. . .

As if in response, Eilidh squeezed his hand.

'I said, "It is my turn now"', she laughed, seemingly as happy as him, but a little nervous. 'Where were you just now?'

Walt reddened, whispering 'I was just thinking of last, last. . .'

Eilidh smiled 'Last night. But It won't be our *la*st, Walter darling. But I have to go. They are calling me. But we'll have a wee bite at the break, back at the cottage. Maybe even have something to eat as well,' she giggled, taking a few steps backwards mouthing him a kiss then turning and running towards the growing chants and rhythmical hand claps.

'*Dom-in-ie! Dom-in-ie! Dom-in-ie!*

The eager, laughing, crowd parted to allow Eilidh passage to the central area. She suddenly leapt aside to allow a tired bull to be led away. The bull despite its swathed horns had apparently been successful (as always) in preventing its tumescence being 'ringed' by any of the young participants' hand- held hoops.

The younger of those exhausted, excited youths, dressed in nothing but a crude hessian loincloth, were now forming in front of a stocks where Eilidh's head now appeared secured in place.

Walt later found that it was Eilidh's annual trial by some of her pupils that was to begin. If she didn't answer any question correctly the pupil was allowed to squash an evil smelling cheese pie in her face.

The MC, a woman of middle years with twinkling eyes announced:

'First Question! One question per year! First Year winner first. Fiona McCaulay!

The crowd cheered and clapped.

'Yes you, Fiona McCaulay' the MC prompted.

A shy young girl dressed in the school unisex taupe woollen smock, shoved forward by what looked like her older brother, suddenly found herself in front of the trapped face of Eilidh. Eilidh smiled her encouragement and said with a stage whisper that just reached through the hushing silence of the crowd as far as Walt on the outer circle, 'Go on, Fiona, don't be scared, we all know it's your first time. Now, what would you like to ask me? You know you can ask me anything…'

'Please, miss, why are you sae bonny?' she blurted.

The crowd roared with laughter. Eilidh laughed too, 'I dinnae ken, Fiona, I suppose-'

Dinnae ken! Dinnae ken! Pie! Pie! Pie! The happy crowd chanted.

The wee girl's bigger brother handed her a large squishy yellow pie and took great delight in leading with his hands filled with the squelchy pie to fully confront a faux-scowling Eilidh. Between the two children they covered Eilidh's squirming face, the boy delightedly and roughly, his younger sister reluctantly and gently spreading the mess.

The crowd encouraged and cheered.

'Ewan McCaulay! First thing Monday morning, my office!' Eilidh spat through a mouthful of runny cream cheese, but her eventual wet grin betrayed any severity.

The crowd as one burst into happy shouts, a mixture of: 'oohs and aws' then a half-hearted chants of:

'The tawse! The tawse! Ewan's fur the tawse! Eee o ma daddy o-'

'Quiet! Next question!' The homely MC barked, wiping the tears of laughter from her face.

Eilidh successfully fielded the next five questions, grateful that they demanded routinely factual answers.

The crowd simulated its disappointment at each correct response.

'Last question! Leaving Year. Rory Anderson!'

A tall skinny acne riddled boy strutted to enjoy his centre stage moment that he finally won in the school's annual competition for 'Asking The Question'. Rory seemed to be suddenly hesitant as he looked around him in the growing murmurs of the crowd's annoyance -- no doubt more than ready to fill the inn with orders for the day's free drink. A thought began to peck at Walt's lovestruck mind, an irk demanding attention that he was needed somewhere else, but it was suddenly squashed with the realisation that the whole crowd were following this young man's eyes, now his rising pointing finger as Rory seemed to have made up his mind and asked of his target:

'Dominie. Who is that?'

Eilidh's clamped head did not allow her to see, but she knew who sleekit, vengeful Rory would be referring to.

'I cannae say, Rory-'

'Pie! Pie! Pie' a delighted crowd roared.

Rory duly gladly obliged and the laughter built but suddenly waned as a fierce cry rang out. They all knew who it was.

The Frugal.

Madder than ever. And he was making straight for him. The Stranger. The Outsider, who had been working in Frugal's howff for about two months...

'There ye are ya wee shirking bastard! Who gave you permission to enjoy yerself! And where's ma phequin front door key?!'

CHAPTER 15: GOODBYE & HELLO (again).

FRUGAL WAS CHASING him, threatening to thump him with a bicycle pump, Eilidh was tied up in the cellar, Walt tugged at the shut cellar door hatch. He tugged and tugged and tugged again. It was stuck fast. Frugal banged him on the back of his head.

Walt woke with a start, feeling the back of his head and wondering about the significance of a big black bicycle pump being part of his nightmare.

He felt as tired as when he had collapsed into bed, what felt like seconds ago. Frugal had manhandled him back to make the inn ready for the evening onslaught of customers of all ages both genders, normal pub rules being suspended until midnight. The Drumhumble bairns made the most of it, all enjoying the sight of a thoroughly scunnered Frugal serving them their soft drinks.

The racket still reverberated in Walt's skull but was quickly subdued by the image of Eilidh. The nearest he had been to her was the width of the street as the village engaged in the Final Event: North versus South. To Walt, the only spectator, (even Frugal joined in, not surprisingly whole heartedly kicking, gouging and punching, but no biting due to his dodgy teeth) the activity consisted of two teams, the sides determined by which side of the one street the person resided.

They had lined up eagerly awaiting a disembodied whistle and the tiny ball that had been thrown in the air – presumably by the phantom whistler. Then pretty much the majority of hell broke loose as the mobs of about one hundred per side tried to usher the wee ball to their respective goals at either end of the street.

Walt was saddened by his last sight of Eilidh seemingly as engrossed in this mad annual blood-letting, as the others. Had she forgotten all about him? She seemed to. Was the dream over?

Soon after the final whistle — a draw was declared, 0-0 the apparent score, then all of the participants had crammed into the inn or so it seemed to an overwhelmed Walt.

Except Eilidh.

Walt and Frugal and Adonald were kept serving until Frugal bawled:

'Midnight! Hame! The phequing lot of ye!'

Walt got to bed after two hours of clearing the wreckage and tidying up, too tired to do anything but hopefully dream of Eilidh. Positive dreams, he prayed. He was wrong: it was one interminable nightmare where he lost Eilidh to Frugal and received a beating from a bicycle pump in the process.

He dragged himself to the inn's kitchen.

Adonald was there sitting at the table a mug of tea steaming in his hand. He was unusually cheery, a result of the rattling applause he had received for the 'turn' he had performed in the packed bar last night. His daft parodies had gone down a storm.

'Breakfast?' the old man asked nodding, indicating the usual selection of fruits, yoghurt and cheeses and bread. 'Ah could fry ye some eggs. . .'

'Coffee will do, thanks.' Walt sat as Adonald poured. Another first.

'Ye really like the Drumhumble Green Mountain, aye ah've noticed. . .best beans for yonks, yer lucky ye arrived this year.' Adonald looked directly at him. Another first, followed by yet another, the old man seemed to be *inviting* a *response*.

Goodbye & Hello (again)

'Grand night, aye.' Adonald supped, smiled and looked at Walt expectantly.

'Aye.' Walt was in no mood for conversation, his tired mind had only one thought: Eilidh.

But the old man was positively loquacious this morning.

'Aye a suitable send off. Cannae complain. Wouldnae do any guid if ah did though, would it?' Adonald hugged his large tea mug with both hands and continued to speak as much to himself as his reluctant audience of one, his gaze turning towards the one small window.

'Aye, the Granny will be getting the Adonald Medicine ready soon. She'll have a label on it by now, so's she disnae mix The Medicines up. Ah ken, she cannae kid Adonald, no as daft as Ah might appear. . .ye notice things at ma age. . .more and more. . .as well as forgetting ither things. . .aye. .. and Granny's she's getting auld jist like. . . forgetting things, jist like the rest o' us. . .aye, the label, 'Adonald's Farewell' Ah bet-- if Ah could -- Ah wid have written a tune tae go with it, a sprightly cheery wan no like thon dreary 'Macpherson's Farewell'. . .Ah could aye ways dae a parody. Parodies are ma speciality, ye ken.' The old man looked away from the window and faced Walt as if suddenly remembering he was there.

Walt wasn't exactly sure what the soliloquy had been about. He had, strangely enough, grown a bit fond of this old, previously taciturn, geezer.

'They went down a bomb, Adonald. Very much appreciated by one and all?'

'Whit? Whit ye oan aboot noo? See you English, ayeways talking roon aboot things, too poncing polite tae come tae the-'

'Your parodies-'

'Ye talking about last night. . .ma performance?'

'Outstanding.'

'Ye really *liked* them? You? Ah mean, did ye unnerstaun them? Ah mean-'

'Most of the references and the language. After my crash course behind the bar, I get most of the words. The majority anyway. . .'

'Ye *did* like them, then?'

'Terrific.'

'Whit one did ye like best?'

'Hard to say. They were all great...'

'C'mon. . .'

'To me. . . well. . .it was a close thing between the *'Save the Last Dance* – sorry *Cans* and the *Birth of the Blues-*'

'Booze. No, Blues. Booze.' The old man sang *'and Drumhumble gave birth to the booze'* his voice as ever, reedy but pure.

'Yeah, that one. . . and the Fleetwood Mac one-'

Adonald took the cue and launched into the parody of *Don't Stop* and its hooky chorus of *Yesterday's Gone.*

'Yesterday's Scone. Yesterday's scone. Don't start asking for today's.

Walt laughed and clapped.

'Aye, well, Ah'll gie ye that, ye have got taste. They were my best three...' A chuffed, chuckling Adonald put down his mug. His face grew serious as he turned to the window. After apparently taking time to choose his words, perhaps finding them in the late morning sunshine streaming in, he spoke:

'For an Englishman, ye ken, yer no' bad. Ye've mair than pullt yer weight in here. . .and that despite the hard time Freaky Frugal has meted oot. . . Ah dinnae ken where ye came fae, why yer here or whit Frugal has in mind for ye and Ah dinnae want tae ken. . . though Ah kin guess it'll be somethng tae dae wi' being ma *successor*.. . if that's the right word.'

'Successor?' Walt had to 'ken'.

'Oh, Ah ken Adonald will be a hard act to follow. . .but time is. . .old age comes to awbody.'

'May I ask how old-'

'Ye no' been listening? I am 74-'

'75 next month!' Frugal unnoticed, had come in and stood at the door listening for some time. He had heard enough.

 'Sorry to break up the mutual admiration society but Granny Mulch wants to see you right now!'

The old man began to rise, spluttering 'But it's no' time yet-'

'No, you! *You*!'

Adonald sat.

Walt rose.

CHAPTER 16: DEAL OR NO DEAL.

1.

Be Prepared (the last Boy Scout)

WALT THOUGHT HARD about taking this chance of going to see Eilidh first, and responding to this summons of Granny Mulch afterwards. He knew his love would not be teaching, she would be at home, it was Recovery Day, the day after Daft Eedjits Day. Walt wanted to 'recover' Eilidh; he wanted to explain why he hadn't come to her last night, that he wanted to but was simply completely exhausted with the overwhelming bar work.

Oh, how he dearly wanted to see her as soon as possible. Had she been offended by his absence? Would she finally answer all the questions he had for her? If she didn't, did he care? – maybe not really, as long as he had her company and her bed to share.

Let Granny Mulch answer his umpteen questions and leave him free to leave Eilidh free to. . .yes!

This time it would be different, aware of, if not wise to, the old woman's sophistry and her avoidance of answering questions; he was stronger too, he felt nothing would be too much for him as long as he had Eilidh. Thoughts of Eilidh warmed and clad him as he realised he was not having to fight off the previously threatening clinging foliage in the lane that led up to Granny's secluded home. (Only later did he ascertain that the triffid qualities of the plants depended on whether Granny *wanted* to see you.) He was determined the get the questions, *his* questions answered by Granny Mulch over and done with, then he would go and be with Eilidh.

He was steeled for Granny as he made to knock on the door.

Yes, he was ready when-

'Come in, Walter. I am ready for you.'

2.

Don't drink the tea

It was a different Granny Mulch Walt felt he faced across the large kitchen table: friendly, like the cat that now jumped up to stand and purr contentedly on his knees, its bodily vibrations making Walt's knees feel queer. He thought he didn't like cats, he was sure he didn't, but that was before. . .before Drumhumble. Drumhumble, where everything was different. He tentatively stroked the cat. The cat responded by sitting, curling and snuggling fully into his lap emitting even louder purrs as it looked up at the open bird cage. The cockatoo screeched, flew out of its cage, and made a bird-line to Walt's right shoulder to land and begin whispering coos in his ear.

'Who's a pretty boy? Who's a pretty boy?'

'Walter, you are really popular.' Granny sipped something from a huge, pewter mug. 'Your charm knows no bounds. First our beloved dominie and now these two. . .'Granny Mulch cackled heartily, proud that her troops were obeying her commands but well aware that her pets' rivalry could quickly overheat, run out of control, and end up being counterproductive to softening up puir wee lovestruck Wally. Their competition for her favouritism she had often used to her advantage. But that was in the past. Now it had become wearisome and wearing. . . *Past it*, she was feeling more and more each day. She must seize the chance that this wee Englishman could offer.

Walt was busily wondering and worrying at Granny's knowledge of Eilidh and himself.

Toby put his purr into overdrive, silently cursing his inability to talk in front of Humans not like that bloody bird chatting up The Outsider, but the sudden swelling under him was some compensation. He would show that oversized Ozzie budgie once and for all who was the Granny Mulch one true familiar. And favourite.

Walt felt like he was receiving a lap massage, he tried for once to *not* think of Eilidh as his face flushed as his trousers tightened at the crutch.

'Off, Toby! Cage Cocky!' Granny gently bowfed. She knew too well what was afoot (and alap).

The bird flew to its cage as the cat slithered off of Walt's lap to curl itself over his clogs. (That second shoe of Walt's was lost forever drowned in the dreaded Dread, so going native was compulsory.)

Toby was content to listen to the feeble protests of the re-caged bird, sulking on its perch balefully eyeing Toby's new position.

'Doing as telt. Doing as-'

'Wheesht! Haud yer wheesht. Or a 'doing' will-', Granny caught herself and smiled at Walt. 'Pets, eh, more bother than they are worth, sometimes.

'Tea, Walter?'

Walt had begun to feel light-headed, what with the bird, the cat, recurring thoughts of Eilidh. . .maybe a mugful of tea would help?

Big mistake. The cat knew.

Toby could have told him if he wasn't muted (and neutered) and Cocky could have if it wasn't so feather-brained and so far up Granny's arse.

3

Staff Training

Toby knew Granny was killing a few birds with one stone. If only the cockatoo was one of them. . .

The cat was all ears: Toby felt that both he and the Outsider were being lectured, instructed, a familiar cat's instinct told him he was an important part of The Plan Granny was laying out. Somehow it smacked of a blueprint to be adhered to after. . .after Granny was gone. . .surely not. Not Granny. . .?

But the more Toby listened the more the cat was convinced. That her Plan might not include herself. At the start he wondered if Granny was just having fun, like on his last visit, playing silly buggers with the Outsider – he should learn to call him Walter if they were to be 'partners', or, Pussy Heaven forbid, if Walt-er was to be the familiar's new *Master*.

But Granny had not been toying with Walter -- not tormenting him like a cat with a mouse. Not prolonging the kill, the kill in this case being the secret ingredients in Walter's tea and the spell she would finally utter thus erasing all memory of her revelations and The Plan. If things didn't work out. . .

No this was not for fun. This was for Real.

It had in essence been a monologue as Granny had anticipated all Walter's questions, then objections.

So, Walt learned and Toby heard the history, some of which, Toby had gleaned in his many years alongside his Mistress but some bits had been new, especially her motivations and beliefs that underlay her many magical actions. Like how she had come to love Drumhumble, being initially grateful for its refuge and due to her longevity and continuity quickly assuming the role of Protector

The Granny State of Drumhumble

(*Protectrix* she called it), culminating in her proudest, most difficult creation The Shield (aka *Scutum*).

Walt learned that Granny had 'naturally' rounded off this task by 'infiltrating' the water supply to gradually erase Drumhumblers' memories of pre-Scutum days and what life was like Outside.

And with the *Scutum* came the myriad benefits: climate control; abundant varied crops; exotic fruits; health, well-being and if not happiness then contentment. A kind of cherry-picked communism, from each according to their nurtured abilities to each the same *essential* needs that were *identical*, all fuelled in no small part by the pirated free electricity via the nearest Outside windfarm.(1)

'But what about emergencies? What about cancer?. . What about Religion. . . What about-' Walt was determined to get the full story, and Granny appreciated that. He had ticked another box, she chackled to herself thinking about his now completely forgotten and abandoned Tik Box enterprise. She knew she had nearly won, they were in the final minutes. Now for the clincher. Ask him *The Question*.

But her hubris got in the way. And her failing short-term memory didn't help. . .

'Emergencies we deal with. Wee ones Frugal takes care of. Big ones I deal with. Who would *want* to be flown to a *hospital*? To catch something unimaginable?

Cancer? What's that? Our diet, the best and purest of fruits and vegetables. And honey from *protected* bees! Aye . . .Mediterranean Diet -pah! With *our* olives. . .so nae obese weans and nae decrepit eh. . .aye, and the complete avoidance of phequing plagues like the 2020s. . . Not that you would remember being born in 20 something – February 28th if memory serves. . .now where was I?. . .Aye. . .

'Religion?! Don't talk to me about they Real Fairy Tales. . . Why would I, eh we, give that house-room? The cause of nearly every war, fight, skirmish, punch up. . .all still endemic and pandemic wherever religion is putatively *tolerated and bluidy rampant! Absolute phequing bluidy nonsense!'*

She calmed a little, catching her breath. 'The last to go from here were the clinging Wee Frees. . .and what a joy that was seeing the erse-end of them. . .a great pity they didn't turn round, back, and see what *joy* actually looked like. . .now what was I saying? Aye. Drumhumble doesn't have a border it has the Scutum.

'Who wouldn't want to live here, Walter? Why would anyone want to leave? And dinnae gie me any of that keech about ma Drummers no having any Freedom. They have complete Freedom. Freedom from all the Outside bad health and rotten weather and plagues and okay we have to forego the luxuries of so-called *choice* that Outsiders enjoy. Choice, my erse!...like 250 different flavours of naffing tattie crisps or chuffing ice cream. . .that's A *TYRANNY* OF CHOICE, THAT'S NEVER FREEDOM! Granny paused, relieved that her Walter had not picked up on the last bee-in-her- bonnet rant. He was not going to counter her *Freedom From* assertions with any questions about the restrictions on *Freedom TO*. She sped on, vowing yet again to watch her runaway tongue.

'Who in their right mind would want to go Outside?' Granny swatted away the disturbing picture of her Fergus this very minute packing his things for his week Outside and smartly smiled at Walter. *Her* Walter now. . .? Now, Nikki, ask THE BIG QUESTION:

'DO YOU-?'

But for once Walt cut *her* off:

'Why have I not seen any old people here. In Drumhumble? Really old, I mean. . .'

Granny felt she had underestimated him. Another plus for her Walt, she wondered, her 749 year old mind racing. . .

The Granny State of Drumhumble

'Me?' she settled for asking, playing for time. For the *right* time to ask her BIG question.

'No I mean-' Walt was still scared. Granny of course knew this and appreciated it.

'-like *normal*?' she laughed.

'Well, yes. Normal Drumhumblers. I mean there are. . .even Adonald is not *that* old-'

'Seventy-five next month! Seventy-five next month! Bye bye barman! Bye bye-'

'Wheesht!' Granny spat. Then sprachled for the cage cover.

Toby hissed and arched his back as he rose up off of Walt's shoes. That cuckoo Cocky! The cockatoo cocking up things as usual. In the Brave Old World Granny might depart and leave behind, if Toby had as much to do with it as he hoped that mouthy bird would be the first in the pot.

CHAPTER 17: NINE MONTHS LATER
(near enough)

GRANNY MULCH PLACED the wee clip gently in place and carefully swathed the incipient belly button in disinfected gauze. Births were a doddle for her these days -- even at Eilidh's age, even at *her* age -- well she had a few bad centuries practice under her antiseptic smock. Melding that experience with gleaned modern obstetric advances she still felt unusually satisfied as she looked down at the brand-new baby boy lying in the splendidly crafted crib.

Granny smiled.

Perfection.

As predicted.

Perfect. Like her Plan and this almost the last part of it. Perfection.

She lifted the swaddled mite and tip-toed to the too big bed that nearly filled the one bedroom in the too wee, twee cottage. The cottage would be needing an extension built gey soon. She needed to take a note of that. At least her wonky memory had reminded her to bring her New Notebook. She would need to take it every time she went out. Unlike best clothes her new notebook wouldnae only be for funerals.

Eilidh was asleep, Granny's knock out mix to remove the barbaric birth pains (imagine these days still going through *that* without a wee something!) was still working. Granny laid the baby next to his mother, took out her wee notebook and a tiny pencil from the one big front pocket in her smock and wrote '*McNulty: extension for Dominie*'.

The Granny State of Drumhumble

She replaced the notebook and pencil and took a wee moment to enjoy the sight of the peaceful duo. Mother and son. Both asleep. One in blissful innocence, the other simply in bliss.

Granny mumbled her wake up words and gently prodded Eilidh. Eilidh's sleepy smile gradually evolved into a face full of joy when she saw what lay next to her.

'Is-' Eilidh began.

'A boy. As predicted. And in full working order, dominie.'

'Thank you, Granny. Thank-'

'No need. All good things come to those who. . .those who deserve it.'

And she did. Deserve it. Granny knew she was too weak regards Eilidh. Granny tried not to get too attached to those who. . .to normal mortals. It seemed like no time at all until. . .look at Adonald, here one minute gone the next. . .But Eilidh had always been special, precious almost, to Granny. . . nearly the daughter she would never be able to have. Like Fergus was the son she mostly indulged. . .and sometimes schooled. . . she had cackled and chortled, yes, chackled and laughed out loud for hours at the sight of him knocking at the Scutum for ages, literally begging her to allow him back in. A day early!

Perfection.

'What about Walter?' Eilidh began to enquire, 'What-?'

'Getting what a new faither needs. A wee dose of the worries. . .Ah thought the yapping of that bloody auld dog of yours might have wakened you and. . .do ye have a name for him yet? And dinnae tell me its Angus-'

Nine Months Later (near enough)

'Hector.' Eilidh beamed down on her son, now cradled in her arms. 'After my father. God rest him. He would have loved to be alive to see this, Granny.'

'Aye. Ah dare say.'

The outside yapping increased; the growls became louder.

'Would you listen to that damned dog! It really does not like yer man. What's happened there? (Later she would recall *precisely* what happened there and where and when and how and why) Ye'll need tae fix that. The dog will. . .when sheepdogs get past it. . .they should be-'

'Never! Angus is-'

'It might be *Angus*,' Granny screwed up her lined and wrinkled (and green) face, 'or Walter.'

'I'll sort it. You don't have to do *everything*, Granny.'

'*If only*,' Granny sighed and mumbled to herself, before saying 'I better let him in, he's suffered enough. And I am talking about Walter. Walter! You can come in now!'

Granny had watched Father Walter come in, turn into a swirling pot pourri of relief, joy, wonder, bemusement, not knowing where to sit, now his clumsy fumbling to hold his baby son safely, then properly.

Granny not for the first time had forebodings if her Plan would really work. It all depended on Wally being Walter. *Her* Walter. And look at him now. An ecstatic lost soul. But then she reminded herself of how well he had come through all of his 'journey.' Then she included her self-congratulations, wholeheartedly deserved, in her view.

Her 'three birds with one stone plan', that now could be *four*! From fixing the Drumhumble gene pool, fulfilling Eilidh and appeasing Fergus's daft notion for a holiday. Wally had been a central figure – a real father and a surrogate innkeeper. . .but now? Maybe. . .

Granny forced her runaway mind to slow as she sat on the one chair the room allowed. The happy trio engrossed on the bed were oblivious to her. At least that damnable dog had quietened. She wanted this peace to think through the last of her Plan, with no canine or feline or avian interruptions for once. The last piece in the jigsaw. . .

She remembered too well how she had started it; her contacting her soul sister, Sonya (actually a fourteenth cousin five times removed in Norfolk.) Something in Granny, call it symmetry perhaps, had led her back for the solution to Norfolk, where she herself had come into the world. Sonya had been another of Granny's prescient inspirations. Sonya's rapid research -- Granny could not believe the speed of discovery -- turned up the ideal candidate for Granny, one Walter Wilson Winston. Sonya, being a couple of hundred years younger than herself was a whiz on something called the Internet. This apparently came into being after Granny's will had created the Scutum which according to Sonya buggered up any chance of any witch, never mind one Granny's, age of using it.

Anyway, between them, the two witches planted the fake abominable reviews on this Internet thingummy on what Sonya termed 'Wally Winston Wilson's Wonderful Web or WWWWW'. Sonya had laughed. Granny had not got the joke, but they had got Walter off his *geeky* (Sonya called it) arse, into his beloved Mazda, up here, into and out of the River Dread. . .Granny stopped her reminiscing about her and her Walter's attainments and made a written note to herself to recover Walter's belongings and fully destroy the wreck of the Mazda.

She began her recollections again. . . through the Scutum. . .and here he was about ten months later. . .having passed every test – especially the Fergus test. Yes, most definitely that.

Since a suitably chastened and thoroughly harrowed Fergus had returned with his tail between his legs, no, up his hubristic arse more

Nine Months Later (near enough)

like, Walter had quickly taken command of all necessary everyday Drumhumble operations. And the villagers responded to his 'carrot' rather than Fergus's 'stick' treatment. Walt, as he liked to be called, was almost accepted. He would be soon enough. In as little as a generation or so.

Granny had prescient worries that her Fergus would return to the opposite side of his hypomania: his normal ferocious self would erupt once she took Walter permanently out of the inn. *The Frugal* could only continue for so long, crestfallen, quietened and subdued by his horrendous experiences Outside. And he would be looking for scapegoats. The whole village would be under siege from Frugal's misplaced wrath. But especially 'The Wally' that had. . .

Yes, now she and the village had seen how Walter's innate good nature and gentle manner had worked, she would need to slip Fergus more than a 'wee something'. His previous belligerence, aggression and downright badness was deep in his blood: his Nature and her Nurture, a combination at the time she felt necessary to control her Drumhumble.

She was a Big Enough Witch to recognise she had been wrong. Probably Fergus appeared on her doorstep at the same time as her Powers began to go and the Fear had over-ridden her usual Good Practice and Husbandry.

Anyway. . .Now she would permanently alter, yes, *modify Frugal*, make him the *Fergus* he could have been.

She smiled over at an oblivious Walter looking as innocent as the child he was petting.

Granny would seize this serendipity. There was no way she was wasting her Walter on quotidian administration. . . another 'double whammy' as Sonya would term it, at least *another* two birds with this one stone, called Walter.

The solution to her fading powers when her time finally came to an end.

Her successor.

She would show that Sonya: get Walter's 'Internet gear' out of the River Dread, get him to train her -- a wee bit anyway -- migraines notwithstanding. She was sure this could only bolster her memory and expand her scrying; then she would train him in things much more magical.

But first things first.

She dug into her huge smock pocket and produced a small crudely wrapped parcel.

Walter and Eilidh looked up, their faces as beatific as ever, as she approached them. She handed over the parcel to Eilidh.

'Blue for a boy. Your boy. Blue. . . For centuries it used to be pink. . .hard to keep track at my age. . .they gin makers. They made a special pink gin for teeny Old Victoria's first child. Turned out to be a girl so it became pink for girls there and then. . .anyway have to dash. Funeral to see to. Well done the pair of you.'

All of a sudden, Eilidh sat up slightly, groaned, now loud and long.

Walt panicked. 'Granny!'

Granny didn't panic. But she did curse herself. More proof of her getting past it. . .

'Out, Walter! Now! And put the big kettle on!'

'What. . .what is it?' Walt asked.

But   the   two   women   knew.

EPILOGUE come CODA

FORTY MINUTES LATER Granny shut the happy couple's front door, failed to land a big boot on Angus and started hurrying to conduct the cremation that was now nearly an hour late.

She started chackling as always at the downright inefficiencies of the human race. Even the so-called Royals could not predetermine the sex of their new borns, never mind arrange it like she could; now that was proper Determination. Pre-determination. Predestination. Oh aye. . .

Control was everything.

From the Cradle to the Grave.

But, for all her scrying she had not foreseen *twins*. The sister for Eilidh's first born. She rubbed her hands. Now her Plan was more perfect if that was possible. *Pluperfect!* She laughed out loud at her Latin pun but more at the Fates being truly kind to her in her final days.

But it was *umpteen* more years she wanted now. At least the twelve or so to see this newly born lass reach her 'bloods' and fulfil the destiny Granny had just 30 minutes since bestowed upon her.

Pluperfect indeed. Witches were so much more caring, empathetic and less selfish than young Warlocks or Wizards blinkered by their machismo egos.

A *Witch* seeing and scrying The Big Picture was what the community of Drumhumble had always needed and a Witch is what it would now get again.

A new *Protectorix*.

The Granny State of Drumhumble

In the meantime, she and Walter would *manage between them*. Her magic and his rescued machine. . .she knew that as the future was now safe she wouldn't have to go to all the exhausting bother and maybe impossibility of training Walter in *her* magic. . .at her age. . .with her migraines. No! Now she could ease into 'retirement' with Walter and his thingummy. . .Computer.

Despite her joy she chackled evilly at the woes and travails the new father would have when this new lass of his reached puberty. Normal lassie teenagers were bad enough trouble at that age. But this one. . .and with a twin for sibling rivalry. . .Eilidh and her 'boys' were in for some treat!

She eventually stopped laughing. Now for this funeral. . .

This funeral, like all Drumhumble funerals and births, Granny had to attend personally: births, to speak her magic words over the babe to further determine their life and lot in the village, whereas funerals still needed, again, her *words* -- they were all cremations. . .now if only she could get them to *self-*combust on the day of their seventy-fifth birthday. Then her retirement would be so much less labour intensive. . .

She would put that put that down on her *To Spell List*.

Granny stopped and took out her new notebook and deep in thought stared at its title:

From the Cradle to the Grave.

Then she casually flipped forward through the subheadings:

Conceptions and Cremations.

THE END.

If you enjoyed this you may also enjoy…

The Sequels:

1) Six hellish gay days Out(side) by Frugal McDougal.
2) The Travails of WWW with a teenage daughter Witch.

TRANSLATIONS, EXPLANATIONS, EXPANSIONS AND ASIDES.

Chapter 1:

(1) brae: *hill* – Walt had quickly mugged up in his *Idiots Guide to Scottish Idioms* before setting out from Norfolk and was determined to use them on his research trip.

Chapter 2:

(1) hoaching: *fidgeting* - always extreme and always physical, sometimes also mental – Walt was destined to hoach a lot during his adventure.
(2) Latin was not only a doddle to Granny; it had once been compulsory not 'dead' like nowadays; okay. . . lawyers, doctors and priests and charlatans and poseurs and flaneurs still use Latin for obfuscation (and expensive billing) but it had been Granny's *first* language for over her 700 years.
(3) glaikit: – various spellings –*unbelievably stupid and otiose.*

(4) Not true. . .but who cares? Granny wanted to believe it. The Myth is mightier than the Word.

(5) Home grown in her fruit and vegetable, spice, herb, and moly garden – the main product plus of her Scutum being Climate Control that required her daily -- chiefly nocturnal – manipulation.

(6) The mere 9 lives of 'normal' cats was yet another urban myth – bucolic too -- probably invented to cause less fright to humans. Or envy. Or dread.

Chapter 3:

(1) Drumhumblers could never agree (unlike the French) on the gender of their twin peaked mountain. Hence the name, *Ben Her.(Aka Marilyn; aka Munros.)*
(2) Scunnered: *really unhappy; sickened, well pissed off.*
(3) Dreich: *overcast; dull;* always applied to weather and usually when at least gently raining. (The Irish equivalent is *soft.*)

Chapter 4:

(1) eedjit: *idiot* but in Drumhumble by 2060 eleven times worse than a 'normal' idiot or eedjit.
(2) sleekit: *underhand <u>and</u> cunning*; – think nearly all politicians and copywriters. . .oh aye, and estate agents. . .as for estate agents who write their *own* copy, *sleekit* would only be half apposite.
(3) nyaff: *inconsequential, insignificant* - usually small in stature, usually annoying, usually male person. . .think Arthur Askey or Ronnie Corbett)

Chapter 5:

(1) Masons only: there were only two of them and all of Drumhumble knew who they were. As for Eastern Star, she kept herself to herself.

Chapter 6

(1) Granny Mulch, Frugal's surrogate mammy had seized the opportunity presented by the Forces of Synchronicity and Serendipity to make her regime more predictable and controllable and this day old foundling whose every thought and deed she could jalouse (figure out) would be her urgently needed 'fist of iron' in her 'velvet glove' -the start of her new F.I.R.M., with its FIRM foundation now laid. So, she named the wee babby boy accordingly – <u>F</u>ergus <u>I</u>an <u>R</u>obert <u>Mc</u>Dougal and further (and improperly) educated him herself. He was special and would not simply receive the utilitarianly minimum schooling with all the other Drumhumble children so she laid special evening and weekend lessons on top of the Three Rs he received from the dominie at the school.

(2) Further on 'the' F.I.R.M. - Granny had given her Fergus the surname McDougal in a fit of irony and as a homage to McDougall's Self-*Raising* product – the true Flour of Scotland.

(3) fernal: *opposite of infernal*. . .why not?. . .time to neologize
a concise antonym. . .you saw it here first.

(4) <u>W</u>ee <u>W</u>alter <u>W</u>ilson <u>W</u>inston's <u>W</u>onderful <u>W</u>ebsite. Granny's sense of irony was never quiet for too long. . .or long enough?

(5) Frugal had the only bad teeth in Drumhumble. He fixed everybody else's but could not fix his own. (You try it, Dear Reader). As for Granny, she refused to help him as she kept her infamous Toothache Spell almost exclusively for 'her Fergus', to keep his worst excesses in check.

(6) chookies: *testicles.*

(7) Eilidh ran the local newspaper *The Drumhumble Drum*, but as it virtually only reported births and deaths (hatches, and despatches -no matches in Drumhumble) as there was hardly any *other news in* Drumhumble, she was never overtaxed.

<u>Chapter 8:</u>

(1) chackling – a 'hybrid' term covering simultaneous *chuckling and cackling.*

(2) stumer*:* <u>see also eedjit</u>; also *warrmer; poultice; bampot; fanny; sumph* -all implying *imbecility or pusillanimity* or *otiosity* or both or all three.*)*

(3) bawbag*:* strictly *scrotum,* but also see last Footnote (2) above for other over and undertones)
(4) mahochmagandy: *sexual intercourse* -- outdoors as well as indoors.

Chapter 9:

(1) muckle: *many or large*, not be confused with *mickle* meaning *small* - the difference encapsulated in the Penny-Pinchers rationalised creed 'many a mickle maks a muckle'.)

(2) uisge-beatha: - various spellings - Gaelic for *water of life* usually served in a 'gentleman's measure'. That is a 'double.' *Whusky*.

Chapter 13:

(1) dwam: *daydream*.

Chapter 16.

(1) Drumhumble's requirements for power were negligible in the scale of Outside things, being mainly for lighting as there was still the predilection of the Drummers for open fires and solid fuel (peat) cooking. And the Scutum made Drumhumble winters non-existent: an actual *verifiable* Greenhouse Effect, despite, or maybe because of, the total recycling of sewage for crop fertilisation and the spin-off of a wee bit of very natural gas in the shape of the allegedly unwelcome methane.

Printed in Great Britain
by Amazon